LOST GIRLS

The Maine Murders

JON MILLS

DIRECT RESPONSE PUBLISHING

Published by Direct Response Publishing

Lost Girls is the first book in the 50 States of Murder Thrillers which was previously published as a Ben Forrester FBI Thriller

Lost Girls: The Maine Murders is a work of fiction. All names, characters, places and incidents either are the product of the author's imagination or used fictitiously. Any resemblance to actual persons, living or dead, events or locales is entirely coincidental.

ISBN-13: 978-1986815178
ISBN-10: 198681517X

Also By Jon Mills

Undisclosed

Retribution

Clandestine

The Debt Collector

Debt Collector: Vengeance

Debt Collector: Reborn

Debt Collector: Hard to Kill

Debt Collector: Angel of Death

Debt Collector: Prey

Debt Collector: Narc

Debt Collector: Hard Time

Debt Collector: Her Last Breath

Debt Collector: Trail of the Zodiac

Debt Collector: Fight Game

Debt Collector: Cry Wolf

Debt Collector: Oblivion

50 States of Murder Thrillers

True Connection

Dedication

For my family.

Prologue

Henri Bruns's house was a secluded property nestled in Big Cypress National Preserve. The sadistic killer who had been terrorizing hikers in the Everglades had eluded the FBI for four years. Thirty-three people had been found dead.

In 2010, a joint task force had been formed to review missing-person cases after a connection had been made to sixteen of the thirty-three who had gone missing in national forests all over the United States. Unlike other serial killers who broke into homes, picked up prostitutes, or snatched their victims off the streets, the animal who the media nicknamed Skinner was methodical and clever.

For years he had continued to go about his murders unnoticed.

Phones rang, officers punched keys, and a large wall was lined with photos of badly decomposed, mutilated bodies.

Ben's hand trembled.

"Are you still with me, Dr. Forrester?" Bruns asked.

At first he didn't believe it. He was sure it was just another one of his games. When he placed Ben's wife, Elizabeth, on the phone, her cries confirmed his worst fear.

"Come alone."

The line went dead.

His supervisor, Nate Mueller, had been the only one who had seen Ben's face turn white after he hung up. Nate tried to get to him before he shot out the door but it was too late. By the time he reached the corridor Ben was already inside the elevator.

"Ben?" Nate called out.

"He has my family."

The doors sealed shut. A few minutes later, sirens blared and lights flashed as Ben fishtailed around a corner, almost losing control of the car. Tires squealed as he gunned the engine. It was foolish, he knew he shouldn't go in alone but this lunatic didn't mess around. Nothing could have prepared him for this. All his years of training and teaching in Quantico was about to be put to the test.

Beside him the phone buzzed. He knew it was Nate. He tapped the button to accept the call. "Where are you?" Nate demanded to know.

"I've got to go in alone."

"Are you out of your mind, Forrester?"

"What other choice do I have?"

Under any normal conditions the FBI would have had a helicopter in the air, a SWAT team ready to move in, and police blocking off every road in a two-mile radius. In the old days Ben would be wired up, but with the latest technology available, "wired" was just an allegorical term. Now they could monitor and record everything through small devices inside the tips of pens, tie clips, or a cuff link. However, today Ben had none of that. All he was packing was his Glock 22.

"Ben, give me an address."

"You already know."

Ben hung up.

Police had raided the home of Henri Bruns two weeks ago after an anonymous tip. Of course he wasn't there but one of his soon-to-be victims was. As much as the local police wanted to take credit for this, it was pure luck, but then catching these kinds of sickos relied on that. The best you could do was hope they screwed up. The joint task force was operating out of Everglades City. From the department it took around twenty minutes to reach his dilapidated excuse of a home.

On US-41 the car reached speeds of over ninety miles an hour, and by the time he pulled on to Burns Road his knuckles were white. All he could feel was rage and fear. How had he managed to get past the patrol car out front of Ben's home? Bruns had broken his method of operation. This had become personal to him.

Approaching the final turn, the car slid as it burst over a rise in the road. Ben barely managed to keep the tires on the ground. His pulse raced and bald cypress trees blurred in his peripheral vision as he stared ahead. Big Cypress was the west part of the Everglades with over a million acres of wetlands. It was grassy, full of slow-moving rivers, marshes, and pine.

Henri Bruns would become the stuff of legends. Only once in a while a serial killer came along that made the others pale in comparison. He had been careful. For the longest time, the bodies discovered were ruled accidents. Hikers who had got lost, wandered into alligator-infested waters, or been attacked by a panther. They still hadn't figured out how he selected his victims or why he wanted them. They just vanished.

For two years Ben had been waiting to catch him.

For two years, he had gone without sleep, fallen into heavy drinking while becoming obsessed with the case.

The car skidded onto the property; Ben's eyes swept

the tree line. Every fiber of his being was on alert. It wouldn't be long before this place would be overrun with cops and feds. He forced his way out of the car and pulled his Glock. He could feel tension in his shoulders as he moved towards the cabin surrounded by red mangroves. Besides the sounds of birds chirping in the trees it was quiet.

He ascended three wooden steps in desperate need of repair. They creaked beneath his shoes. Ben peered through a window. There was no movement inside. Not even a sound. He didn't kick the door open. That kind of action would get you killed. The police tape that had covered the door was on the floor. Someone had been in. He stood to one side, kept his gun lowered, and turned the handle. Over the years he'd seen all manner of lunatics rig up guns that would go off when you walked in. If Bruns's goal was to kill him, it wasn't going to be because of stupidity. Ben swallowed hard as he gave the door a push and it swung open. He cut the side of the door with his head just enough to see if anyone was inside. It was empty.

The smell of smoke from a wildfire started somewhere in Big Cypress Preserve still lingered in the air. Ben eased into the cabin with his back against the wall. He swept the room with his eyes. The place was a dive. Dirt everywhere. They said this was his main residence but Ben didn't believe that. This was where he played. He didn't care how the place looked, only that it was in an isolated part of the preserve. Somewhere they could scream and not be heard.

A white flickering glow came from a room further down the hallway. The bedroom. The victim had been found tied to the bed. Still alive. Unharmed. That's what burned Bruns. That he didn't get to have his sick way with her.

Inside on the bedside table was a tablet. On the screen was the madman himself wearing a Halloween mask of Ronald Reagan. Behind him a blank brick wall. Where was he?

"Ah, glad you finally made it, Dr. Forrester. Or should

I call you Ben?"

"Where are they, Bruns?"

He let out a maniacal laugh. "All in good time."

"I want to see them now."

"You will but first, tell me, how did you know where to look?"

"It doesn't matter."

"Oh it matters to me, Ben."

There was a beat.

"You got sloppy."

Bruns let out a snort. "How so?"

"Enough of your games. Where are they?"

The sound of sirens could be heard in the distance. He paused for a moment staring blankly at the camera.

"Okay, Ben. In front of you inside that box is one key and the coordinates to the location of your family and the lovely Marie Porter."

Marie Porter had been one of two girls missing. She was seventeen, only two years older than Ben's daughter at the time.

Ben cautiously flipped the lid on the old shoebox. Inside was the key, and a scrap of paper with two GPS coordinates. His chest rose and fell fast as he flipped the paper over, hoping to find more than this.

"Which one is for my family?"

"That's for you to figure out, but I would hurry if I was you, Ben, they don't have a lot of time or air for that matter."

"And the key?"

He took a hold of it between his finger and thumb.

"It only releases one of them."

"What?"

He let out a final laugh.

"Bye, Ben."

"No, no, no. Wait."

The screen went black. Ben raced outside with the coordinates in hand, he was immediately met by Nate and a squad of cars. "What's going on?" Nate asked.

Ben was beside himself. He willed himself into thinking clearly. He held out the paper and key, his hand shaking.

"He has them and the girl at these coordinates but we only have one key and no idea which one leads to my family."

Nate immediately took control. He had an officer bring up the locations on a GPS.

"I need a chopper to head to the farthest one and we'll take the swamp buggy to the other," Ben said.

"And the key?" Nate asked.

Ben felt as if he was having an out-of-body experience.

"Ben!"

"Either way someone is going to die," Ben replied.

Both sites were located in remote areas of the Everglades. He was going to kill them the same way. He'd bury them alive. Nate jumped on the radio and gave the coordinates to the eyes in the air.

"Roger that!" a voice said over the radio.

Squad cars raced onto the road heading in the direction of the second set of coordinates. Ben radioed ahead to have two swamp buggies and shovels ready. His mind was going crazy. The thought of never seeing Adam, Chloe, or his wife again was too much to comprehend. No matter how fast they moved, it wasn't fast enough. Every second was a chance they wouldn't make it in time.

It took the better part of an hour to make their way to the spot. The buggy was caked with mud, and their clothes were covered as they arrived at a deserted location near a riverbed with gators.

"Over there," an officer pointed towards a fresh pile of soil. Footprints from vehicle tracks led up to it. Ben pushed off the buggy and raced over. He slammed the shovel into the earth and frantically began heaping piles of soil to one side. Every time he pushed into the thick, moist soil he was waiting to hear the sound of a box. Wooden, metal, plastic, Bruns had used anything he could get his hands on. Over the radio they could hear that the pilot of the chopper was having difficulty locating a place to land.

Ben took another scoop and this time hit metal. It was

a steel box.

"Quick."

He and the others got on their hands and knees and started scooping away handfuls of dirt and wiping the surface to try and find the lock. A moment later, he felt it. He took the key and jammed it in, twisting it. He yanked it off. Once it was unlocked, Nate and another officer helped him pull back the steel lid.

"Careful."

The moment they opened it, Ben knew he wouldn't see his family alive.

Inside the steel death trap was Marie covered in venomous snakes. She was dead. Ben fell on his knees and gripped the soil.

"Tell me you've landed?" Nate said over the radio.

"Boots are on the ground."

The waiting was torturous. They had to shoot the lock on the second box. When they eventually opened it, Elizabeth and Adam were already dead.

Nate looked at Ben and shook his head slowly.

There were no snakes inside but it didn't matter. He would later find out that they had been dead for hours. Coroner said it was a lack of oxygen. Right there and then Ben's world ended. As he wept uncontrollably, Nate was still speaking with the officer on the radio.

"Repeat that?" Nate asked.

"Only two bodies, an adult female and a young male."

Ben looked at him. "What? Chloe is not there?"

It didn't take long to establish where she was. The evening Henri Bruns had taken Elizabeth and Adam, Chloe had been invited to stay over at her friend's house. The only reason she was alive was because of that.

Chapter 1

Eden Falls, Maine, late June 2016

For the past two years, Ben Forrester had lived in a small beach house on Mount Desert Island. At 5 a.m., he breathed in the salty North Atlantic air from his front porch and drank in the sights and sounds that he'd become accustomed to at that hour. Working lobster boats, private sailboats, and motorboats bobbed gently in the harbor. Situated seventy-five feet from rosy granite cliffs were steps that led down to a private cobblestone beach that offered exactly what they needed — peace and seclusion. He could have bought a home overlooking the Gulf of Maine but the view of Frenchman's Bay was spectacular. Besides, Elizabeth's mother lived just a few houses down and what a lifesaver she had been after the funeral.

Dreams had once again been filled with nightmares. It

was difficult to shake the past, even harder to step into the future. Settling into the new town of Eden Falls had become almost a full-time job. Nate Mueller had been on him to return to the bureau over the past year. Nate was sure that he'd eventually wear him down, but Ben didn't have any intention of returning.

That afternoon he had his usual 1 p.m. therapy session with Dr. Emily Rose, a local therapist. He saw her twice a week, sometimes three if the dreams got really bad. She ran her private practice out of a four-bedroom Victorian house. It was the same every time. He would arrive, soft music would be playing. Emily wouldn't enter until the moment the clock ticked over to one.

Ben sat on the sofa across from her.

"So how are you doing today, Ben?"

Ben swept the room, looking at all the certificates she had. It was very minimalistic. Everything had its place. There was no table in the room. Just two soft leather couches. In the first few months he nearly gave up. He'd felt uneasy pouring out his life story to a stranger. He didn't like the feeling that he got or the same questions being asked. How did that make you feel? she would ask and he would just shake his head. She said time was a healer but that hadn't worked for him. It all seemed so pretentious. He wasn't sure what bothered him about the place — whether it was her questions or his attraction to Emily. She was single and had never been married.

Ben cleared his throat, and tried to put into words how he was feeling.

"I guess I'm okay."

"Okay as in coping or not sure how to respond?"

What was it about her that was so disarming? Had it been anyone else he was sure he would have told them to mind their own business and got up and walked out. But he couldn't do that with her. Emily was two years younger than him. At thirty-nine, she had long dark hair, emerald eyes that pulled you in, and a physique that made you look twice. She always wore flats, and a tight dress that showed off her curves. While others might have been looking at the clock, rambling on incoherently about their feelings, he would find himself staring at her lips, or the way she moved. It wasn't a sexual thing. Habit really. He was used to studying people. Everyone had their own little quirks. The way they sat, looked, laughed, or moved. You could learn a lot from a person's body movements.

Emily smiled. It was a warm and inviting smile that only drew him in further. He had already made up his mind that the only reason he showed up was because of her. She had become the closest person to a friend that he had made since arriving in Eden Falls.

"Tell me about him?"

That was one question she wouldn't stop asking. By him, she meant Henri Bruns. She was convinced that if Ben could talk about the man he could move on. But the truth was you never moved on from the loss of a wife or son. You just appeared to. Of course to the outside world you got up, showered, put on clean clothes, and did all the little things that made you seem like you had a grip on reality. But that was all a thin disguise.

"Are you still drinking?"

"Yeah."

"How many?"

"What is this, an A.A. meeting?" Ben snapped before immediately apologizing.

She shuffled in her seat, crossing her legs. She noticed him looking.

"No, it's okay to let it out. Recognizing and allowing those feelings releases them. That's why it's good to talk about him even if you don't want to."

Ben was silent, staring at Emily. The very mention of Bruns made him feel rage and struggle inside. It was always over what he could have done, should have done differently. He often came back to his own shortcomings, as if he could have controlled the outcome, protected them, or seen it coming.

"You said no one knew how he picked his victims, did you?"

His eyes locked on hers. "I had a theory. A hunch if you can call it that. Bruns lived and breathed this. He watched his victims. He knew how police worked. He was careful not to be seen. He wasn't like Bundy who went for women only with a certain hair color. Though he liked women that were young and pretty, you know, the ones that were out of his league. Then again he picked men, but only those who he could overpower easily and fast. The only connection between victims was that they were in the Everglades at the time or a national park. Some were hikers, others camping. They would just vanish. Search parties would be sent out and after five or eight days it would be called off. He didn't care. He'd snatch them by day and by night. He kept changing his method of operation. While we can confirm thirty-three dead, and sixteen positively connected to him, we believe he slaughtered many more over the span of four years."

"Sixteen?"

"Yeah, but he disposed of many more. It's hard to find bodies that are buried alive, or fed to the gators."

"And the ones that weren't found?"

Ben breathed in deeply. He struggled to talk about it. He couldn't even begin to tell her what Bruns had done with the bodies that weren't buried. The FBI never released the information to the media. The sickening act was just too much. He searched for the words to reply when his phone buzzed.

"Go ahead," she said.

Emily didn't press a button on her computer to stop the recording like she did with her other clients. They met on the condition that she didn't record anything he said. It was too dangerous. Henri Bruns had never been caught. He was still out there. The very thought of it burned him.

"Hello?" Ben said.

It was a teacher from Chloe's school. Chloe was now seventeen and approaching her final year of high school.

"Sure, I'll be right over."

He hung up and rose from his chair to leave.

"Everything okay?" Emily asked.

"They want to speak to me at the school. Not sure what it's about."

"We haven't chatted about Chloe, maybe next time."

Ben nodded. He got up and grabbed his gray peacoat jacket off the hook, adjusted his shirt, and was about to leave. He paused at the door.

"Everything remains confidential, right?"

"Of course."

He hesitated before replying. "The ones he kept, I mean, the ones he didn't bury alive — he stripped their skin, and posed them at an exhibit in Florida called Body Works. No one had a clue. The public just assumed the bodies came from donors. They were unrecognizable."

She nodded as a look of horror spread across her face. Then without saying another word Ben left.

Chapter 2

Ben drove on Mount Desert Street, which then changed into Eagle Park Road, and followed it west. He had been called out to the school numerous times over the past year. Mainly it was concern over Chloe not paying attention, speaking back to teachers, and at one time hitting another kid. She said the girl had stolen her camera. Unfortunately, they had nothing to go on and neither did Chloe. It didn't help that the substitute teacher had waited until the end of the day to inform the principal of the incident, by then the kids had gone home.

He brought his window down and rested his elbow on the ledge of the window. A warm summer breeze blew in. He kept his speed to around forty-fifty miles an hour. They were a stickler on the island for the speed limit, and tickets were issued for going over by even a few miles per hour. He'd seen a cruiser partially hidden on Trent Road.

They only had one unmarked squad car, and that was easy enough to spot as it sat lower than other vehicles due to all the gear they carried, and of course there were the lights behind the grille that were a complete giveaway.

One of Ben's initial concerns in moving to Eden Falls was anonymity. He didn't want everyone knowing. Very little got leaked to the media about who was involved in the Everglades case. A reporter by the name of Edwin Parker had hounded the FBI for details around the time the joint task force was set up. The guy was an insect who spent more time hiding in the woods trying to listen in on conversation than doing any real reporting.

For the past year Ben had picked up some work doing remote teaching with police officers and university students looking to understand the mind of a criminal. It didn't pay well, but he still had his old property in Florida that he was renting out.

Ben heard the squeal of a siren; he glanced in his mirror then pulled to the side of the road as a cruiser blew past him. It made him uneasy. In his twenty years with the FBI he rarely found himself speeding to a crime scene except for that one time. Contrary to public opinion, car crashes were what killed most officers. A state of panic and too many vehicles on the road could mean certain death. Not that he hadn't been in his fair share of high-speed pursuits back when he was a cop in Manhattan, but that was a long time ago.

He leaned back in his seat as the world rushed by him. Now he was taking things slowly. He ran a hand through his dark hair that was slowly turning grey. At forty-one he was beginning to show signs of aging. Fine lines at the corners of his eyes, and silver flecks at the sides of his temples. These were the years he was meant to be enjoying married life. Instead he was fighting to keep his head above water.

Reaching into the compartment beside him he fished out a pack of smokes. He'd given up five years ago, but he still kept them handy. He didn't bother with electronic cigarettes; he had no need for them as he never lit these. He took out one and placed it between his lips. That was all he needed. In many ways he was addicted only to having one in hand, the urge to light was gone.

When he arrived at Eden Falls High School he parked out front in the teachers' parking area. Inside he passed a number of students going down the hall. All the lockers on either side were green. There were a couple of students just beyond an exit door smoking. When he reached the main office, he went in and waited to be seen. The woman behind the desk was wearing a red shirt with yellow flowers on it. It was an eyesore but then again so were her shoes, which were bright red. A fat teacher came in and poured himself a coffee from the dregs that were left in a glass carafe.

A moment later, a slender, blond-haired woman who looked as if she was no more than thirty-five came out.

"Please come on in," she said.

Ben followed her into an office. She closed the door. He caught a name on her desk. Meghan Wells, Guidance Counselor.

"What has she done now?"

"She didn't show up today."

The moment she said that fear crept over him. She had never missed school, never missed a lesson.

"But I dropped her off here myself."

"Right, I understand, but quite often kids will wait until their parents have left before they leave."

Ben jumped up. "I need to find her."

"Mr. Forrester. I can assure you this is quite normal." She lifted her eyebrows. "We have a number of students who are in the habit of not showing up. Most of them turn out to be in Acadia Park, or by the lake. Besides, Chloe's friend informed us that's where she would be. I thought it best you know and perhaps you can bring her in so we can all have a talk."

"Where is she?"

Sixty percent of the island was forest; trying to find someone in there without any directions could take you forever. There had been many tourists who had wandered in there and got lost. After hearing those reports Ben had considered moving but Chloe was set on the idea of staying. She wanted to be close to her grandmother. Ben didn't realize it yet but that wasn't the only person she wanted to be close with.

"She said to start with Lookout Point," Wells said.

Lookout Point faced Frenchman's Bay. It was a place that a number of youngsters would go to and make out. The very mention of it sent Ben's mind into overdrive.

"Uh, Mr. Forrester, I wondered if we could…" He didn't catch the last thing she said as he was already on the way out the door.

Since arriving two years ago, Ben had become very protective of his daughter. He knew he couldn't control every aspect of her life but it would have killed him if anything happened to her. She was all he had left. The anchor that was grounding him and keeping him from losing his mind. At seventeen she was bound to want to start seeing guys. He'd started earlier than that, but watching your kid grow up and giving them slack was tough, especially after the way he'd lost Elizabeth and Adam.

* * *

The red, 2003 Pontiac was parked at the far end of a road that had a beautiful view of the bay. Chloe had spent the better part of the day driving around the island with Jake Ashton. It had been the second day in two months that they had skipped school. With one year left and attendance that was almost perfect, she needed a day off from it all.

"God, you're beautiful," Jake said, running his left hand over her face and exploring her body with the other.

"Slow down, there's no rush," she said, squirming at his touch.

Jake peeked out the windows. "But there's no one around. By the way, I have a little bit of…" He pulled out a small metal canister and shook it. "Rum and coke."

"Where did you get that from?"

"My old man."

"Jake, he'll go nuts if he finds out."

He blew his cheeks. "He won't know. The guy is too drunk half the time to know where the bathroom is."

He twisted off the cap and swigged, then handed it to Chloe. She had alcohol enough times, she took a drink and winced. "That's it, get it down, yah." He tipped it ever so gently as she brought it to her lips. A trickle went down the side of her cheek. He licked the side her face.

"Oh gross," Chloe said. Jake just laughed and went back to biting the side of her neck which made her groan a little. When he started undoing her buttons and running his hand underneath her skirt, she began to feel uncomfortable. It wasn't that she hadn't been with a guy before but she wasn't ready to have sex in a car out in the open.

"Come on, Chloe. How long have we been seeing each other?"

"I could ask you the same thing. It's not that I don't want to. I just want it to be..."

"Perfect? Oh please, that crap is overrated. Get 'em off."

Jake started tugging at her underpants.

"Jake. Listen. Not now."

But he wasn't hearing a single word she was saying. In fact, he was so engrossed in kissing and trying to get her clothes off that he didn't hear the truck pull up behind them. By this point she was shoving him trying to get him off. He pressed her hands down and had this wild look in his eyes. He had to have been twice her size and weight. Seeing he wasn't taking no for an answer, she took the one opportunity she had and kneed him in the groin, then followed through with a palm to the nose. He let out a lungful of air, gasped, and grabbed his nose which was dripping blood all over the place. Then like a sudden storm his demeanour changed real quick.

He cursed and forced her arms down when the door opened and he was yanked backwards. Chloe didn't know what was more embarrassing — having her father find her with a guy or seeing him toss the kid like a sack of potatoes.

"What the hell?" Jake mumbled while he cupped his face.

Her father shot her a glance. "Chloe. In the truck

now."

"Oh for god's sake, Dad, I could handle it."

"Yeah, you really looked like you were handling it."

Her father slammed the door, and they left Jake cowering on the ground nursing a bloodied nose.

Chapter 3

The journey home was filled with silence. Ben had peppered her with questions but she refused to answer beyond a nod or a grunt. Ben parked the truck, hopped out, and watched Chloe run into the house. He'd be lucky if he could pull her out of her room for supper. She was wise to his negotiation and interview skills — mirroring body language, matching the same tone of voice. She left the door open and Jinx, their four-year-old German shepherd, came bounding out.

They had got her when she was just an eight-week-old pup. That first month was like hell on earth. It was harder than raising a child. Although the first year felt like a baptism by fire, her training with a local trainer had gone well, and she soon became a great companion that offered protection at night, and friendship by day. She wagged her tail and came up and started sniffing at his pant leg. She always did that. Once satisfied that he'd not been with any other dogs she walked beside him back into the house, occasionally giving him a look as if she could sense trouble.

"Yep, I know, but she doesn't listen, Jinx."

That's what conversation in this town had amounted to, a one-way meaningful discussion with a dog and one hour twice a week with a therapist. He desperately needed some real adult conversation.

Inside, he poured himself a scotch on the rocks and put on some Bach. It wasn't that he liked classical music, in fact he rarely listened to it before he came to Eden Falls. Usually he opted for blues, Muddy Waters, or Buddy Guy, but there was something very soothing about it. He took his computer and took a seat in the sunroom. It was one of his favorite places to sit and watch the sun rise and set over the harbor.

He had to be online at three with the University of Massachusetts to give a talk to students majoring in criminology and criminal justice. It was one of the few universities that let students take a course in counterterrorism. The talks weren't usually long. Two hours at most. It paid okay, and allowed him to not have to step out of the house that much. He would dive into assessing human behavior more than anything else. They all wanted to know the secret. What was the trick to catching a killer? He would tell them the same thing every time.

There was no trick. You had to be willing to go into the darkest recesses of your mind and think like them. Profiling helped but there was no guarantee. You had to be willing to let a case become an obsession.

Most of the universities got in touch with him through his publisher. Prior to taking an extended leave from the FBI he'd published a few books on psychology, criminal profiling, and tracking serial killers.

Jinx padded into the sunroom and curled up around Ben's feet. After getting done with the lecture, he turned on the television and flipped through the news channels. It had become routine. With Henri Bruns still out there, he knew murders wouldn't stop. However, reports of hikers going missing were a common occurrence. The National Park Service didn't have a centralized database of people who went missing. It was the reason why Henri had managed to stay off the radar for so long. It came down to a few things: manpower issues, cost and the amount of time it would take. Most, if not all the disappearances would gain a small, short-lived amount of media attention. A search party would go out for five to eight days at most and then it would be called off. It was only when a couple of hikers found the remains of one of Bruns's victims after a flash flood that the FBI was called in. In many ways he had the perfect hunting ground. National parks were vast, full of bears and mountain lions. If a person hadn't died from being attacked by animals, the elements would get them.

Ben did a search for recent disappearances. A few came up on the West Coast, two in Yellowstone, one in Oregon, and another on the Appalachian Trail. The problem was these were just a few. There were others. There were always others. Those that would never make news sites. It was the randomness of it all. Certainly, some of them were legitimate cases of people who had wandered too far, taken a wrong turn, or been attacked by animals but it was the ones who hadn't. That was what had kept him up late at night as he pored over reports. Ben took a sip of his scotch and felt the blissful burn as he swallowed. He cast a glance out at the tall pines that framed his home. He got up and walked into the garage. There it was sticking out of a box. It was a corkboard that he'd used when the case was first opened. On it was a map of the United States with pins pressed into every area where someone had gone missing. While they were spread out, the bulk of the disappearances were in clusters in and around the Everglades.

He resisted the urge to go and pull it out. It had become a force of habit. Every time a new disappearance came up he would put a pin in it. For the first three months after arriving in Maine he had it on the wall. He barely slept in that time. It took a great amount of urging by Emily to take the board down and take medication for the sleepless nights. Two years later Ben still had problems sleeping but it was better than before. He now got six hours instead of four.

He walked back into the kitchen and shut one of the windows he'd left open that morning. He berated himself as he went through the house checking each of the rooms and closets for anyone who might have got in. This included the basement and the attic. He'd been so careful over the past year but as they found themselves settling in, he was becoming more relaxed. Less guarded, and he wasn't sure that was a good thing.

He opened the fridge and then the freezer above it to see what to cook up for supper. He was so used to Elizabeth doing it. It wasn't that he was averse to cooking, he loved it, but she called the kitchen her domain — the one place she loved to hang out. He paused for a moment looking at the breakfast bar. A memory of Elizabeth in their old house pouring wine while meat hissed on the stove came back to him. Her touch. Her laughter. At least Bruns hadn't stolen his memories. Those were his.

He refilled his glass and shouted up to Chloe.

"You want to get Chinese tonight?"

"We had that last night."

"Seafood?"

"That was the night before."

She was right. Most days it was just easy to pick up food from the local restaurants in town. The place was rich with fish. They had pretty much tasted every kind of fish there was to offer.

"You want to come down, I'm kind of talking to a wall here."

Ben heard her feet patter against the hardwood floors. He couldn't help but smirk when she reached the top of the stairs. Even though she was seventeen she would always be his little girl. Last winter she'd headed off to high school wearing a flimsy jacket and tight jeans. Maine winters were brutal.

"You know you should wear a winter jacket."

"I'm not three, you know," she'd replied back. The memory made him smile. She was growing up fast and it wouldn't be long before she would be heading off to college. The thought was daunting. At least here he could keep an eye on her and protect her.

He waited at the bottom of the stairs for her to come down.

"I don't know what you find so funny?" she said.

"You. You make me laugh."

She rolled her eyes like a typical teenager and walked straight by him. Back in the kitchen she rooted around in the freezer and pulled out a Tupperware container of food that Janice, Elizabeth's mother, had cooked up a few days ago. There wasn't a week that went by that she wasn't dropping off a dish or two. At first, Ben thought it was because she was trying to be kind, he soon learned it was because she'd tasted his home-cooked food. Chloe found it quite amusing.

Chloe turned on some music via her tablet, and gave Ben a hand in the kitchen. While she set the table, he tried to bring up the topic of what had happened earlier that day.

"Look, um…"

"Dad, I get it. You're afraid that something bad is going to happen to me. But you can't wrap me in cotton forever. I know how to handle myself and even if I can't… you've got to give me some breathing space."

"Yeah, I know."

Ben had tried to encourage her sense of independence by teaching her what he knew about hand-to-hand combat. It wasn't anything special, just what he'd picked up in his time in the army as well as what they'd taught them at the academy. At least it gave him some sense of peace that she could protect herself if push came to shove.

"But not showing up to school. No, that I don't give you any room for. I taught you better than that."

"Like you didn't ever take a day off."

"Sure, I might have pulled a sicky or two but my parents always knew where I was. Going off with someone you haven't even introduced me to, well... Do you know how panicked I was?"

"I'm sorry, Dad."

She dropped her gaze to the floor and brought over some iced tea. Ten minutes later they sat at the table eating something that was meant to resemble lasagna. It tasted better than anything Ben could have rustled up. His cooking skills needed some work. Put him in a room with a suspect and he could get into their mind, mess with them, and extract the information they needed. He paused, taking a bite. For all his training and success with others, none of it had worked on Henri Bruns.

There was a knock at the door. Jinx bounded out to the front entrance and began barking like a lunatic.

"Jinx, quiet down."

Ben washed the mouthful of food down with some iced tea and then shuffled over to the door. Beyond the window he saw the police. *Great,* he told himself.

"Chloe, you want to get the dog?"

"Jinxy," she whistled, and he dashed back into the eating area. Once Chloe gave him the okay, he cracked the door open and switched on the outside light so he could see clearer. The officer had light flowing hair, pretty eyes. The kind of woman you would have been happy to introduce to your mother.

"Officer."

"Evening, Dr. Forrester."

"Just, Ben. Call me Ben."

"Right. I'm Officer Woods. I'm sorry to call on you so late but I was wondering if could have a moment of your time?"

She must have expected he would immediately invite her in. She was wrong. "Is there a problem?"

"It's about Jake Ashton."

Ben snorted at the mention of his name. "Sure. Come on in."

Jinx must have got away from Chloe's grip as she had managed to push her way out into the hall. Before Ben could grab her, she was bounding around excited to see a new face.

"Well that's odd. She's usually pretty guarded with strangers."

The woman crouched down.

Oh, I wouldn't do that. Ben had visions of Jinx snapping at the officer's face or knocking her to the ground. The real estate lady who had sold the property had been by a couple of months ago to see how they were enjoying the home. She left with a bruised nose. Jinx had head-butted her pretty hard.

The officer buried her face into Jinx's neck and rubbed behind her ears. Jinx seemed to love it. Her whole body wagged.

"You have dogs?" Ben asked.

"No, but I do have a fish."

He smiled.

"No, I used to have two dogs growing up." She stood back up.

"Chloe, do you want to take Jinx out back?"

"Actually I was wondering if I could have a word with you, Chloe?"

"Is she in trouble?"

"I wanted to get her side of the story."

"Has he filed a complaint?"

"Not yet, but his father was in this evening. It's just what we have to do."

As they waited for Chloe, Ben led the officer into the living area. She cast a glance around the place. "This was the old Mars place."

"That's right," he said.

"You've done a good job on renovating."

"Ah, it still needs some work but we are getting there."

He could tell she was itching to say something and possibly she might have if Chloe hadn't come back into the room.

"Right. Do you want to tell me what happened this afternoon?"

Chloe looked at Ben. She hesitated to reply. He gestured for her to go ahead. She brought her up to speed on what happened. There was a lot of going back and forth, ten minutes later the officer looked as if she had what she needed.

"Do you want to file charges?"

"For what?" she asked.

"Attempted rape?"

She bristled. "No. I don't think he was going to do that. He got carried away."

The officer studied Chloe's face. "Well, if you change your mind, I'll leave my card with you."

Chloe stared at it.

"Anyway, have a good night," Woods said.

Ben led her outside and closed the door behind him. The air outside was clear and smelled of pine. The sound of crickets could be heard as well as waves lapping up against the shore. The officer stepped down from the porch and was about to leave when she turned back.

"Ben Forrester."

She tapped her finger against her lips. "You wrote that book about serial killers. *Inside the Mind of a Monster.*"

His eyebrow shot up. "You've read it?"

"Yeah. I have it in the car, actually." She thumbed over her shoulder.

"Then, unfortunately yes."

She nodded slowly. "I thought I recognized you." She

fixed her gaze on him. "I mean, from the back of the book."

"Yeah, I tried to get them to take that off. But they wouldn't have any of it."

"I don't know, it's not a bad shot." She smiled.

Ben shifted from one foot to the next.

"Well, it was nice to have met you, Officer Woods."

"Dakota, call me Dakota."

Chapter 4

She only wanted to escape.

Twenty-four hours ago, Rachael Taylor arrived at Blackwoods Campground on Mount Desert Island. It was a weekend getaway. Hiking the trails of Acadia National Park. A few drinks with a friend. It was meant to be a place to unwind and let her hair down before returning to the heavy workload that came with attending the University of Maine.

Now it was all about survival.

"Help! Somebody!"

Pain coursed through her as tears blurred her vision. Panicking to get away she stumbled and fell, skinning her knees. Bloodied and scrambling to her feet, she kept running. She had no idea where she was. The forest was almost pitch-black except for light that came from a crescent moon.

Where is he? She cast a fearful glance over her shoulder

while keeping her hands out in front of her. Stone cut into her bare feet, the ocean wind nipped at her exposed skin. Wearing nothing more than panties and a bra, both covered in dirt from falling over countless times, she was freezing.

I just need to make it to the road, she told herself. But she had no idea where she was. Acadia covered over forty-seven thousand acres. Trying to find someone in this place was like searching for a needle in a haystack. How far behind was he? As she staggered forward, her shoulder slammed into a tree trunk. She'd lost count of how many times that had happened. The only thing pushing through her mind was to get away from him. Her throat burned and her heart smashed against her chest wall as she dashed through the dense evergreen forest of tall pines.

"Rachael! Get back here," his gruff voice only made her run faster. She hadn't stopped to look at the deep cuts he'd made in her flesh. His delight in her agony was sickening. Her entire body ached and screamed with more pain than she had ever felt before. It had been so bad that she begged to die, but he wouldn't give her that peace.

She tripped again, this time over a decayed fallen log, and landed face first into the earth. The forest was covered in a thick blanket of lush green moss and ferns. Below it was harsh granite. *Get up.* Shards of light filtered down, piercing the spidery webbed canopy of branches above her.

I don't want to die, she repeated over and over in her mind as she frantically kept her feet going. The will to live and pure desperation pushed her on.

Suddenly, without warning the forest was gone. She burst out on to a single-lane road, panting and gasping for air. Not stopping even for a second to decide whether to go left or right, she rushed towards a faint illumination in the distance. Was it the town? A vehicle approaching? As she rounded a bend in the road, she breathed a sigh of relief. Under the light of the moon, she could see a sign for Eden Falls Harbor. Below it said five miles. She was so close, and yet still nowhere near being safe.

She stumbled and staggered forward, every step excruciatingly painful.

The rumble of an approaching vehicle in the distance was the first glimmer of hope she had felt since escaping the nightmare. She pushed her dark matted hair out of her eyes and gave a cautious look back before pressing on.

A black 4x4 truck shot over the rise in the road with its light bars on full beam. She lifted her hand to block the glare. It was driving at breakneck speed. The roar of its throaty muffler cut into the night.

She began waving. “Please, stop.” She nearly lost her footing as she approached it with little concern that she was in the middle of the road and the truck wasn’t slowing down. Then as its headlights illuminated her, the driver slammed the brakes on. Tires squealed and gravel spit as it swerved to avoid hitting her. She collapsed on the ground, no longer caring if she lived or died. Every ounce of her energy was sapped from her body.

She heard a door creak open, country music seeping out, and then boots hit the gravel.

"Miss, are you out of your mind? I nearly hit you." The closer he got the slower his pace became. "Okay, I'm going to get you some help."

"No!" She pushed herself up on one elbow and reached out for him. "He's coming, please, don't leave me here."

"Oh, it's okay. I'm not going to leave you out here."

He rushed over and she felt strong arms wrap around her waist as he hauled her up. One arm draped loosely over his shoulder, her feet barely making contact with the pavement, she soon found herself in the warmth of the truck.

"Now, don't you worry, miss, I'll make sure no one else touches you," the driver said as he slipped behind the wheel. She could feel herself going in and out of consciousness. Even the smallest light from inside the cab stabbed her eyes.

"What are you doing out here?" he asked.

She tried hard to muster a reply as darkness crept in at the side of her eyes. "I don't know. A man. He was…"

The truck peeled away into the night as she lost consciousness. The last words she heard were, “Don’t worry, you’re safe now.”

Chapter 5

Dakota had a bad feeling about this as she made her way out to Acadia National Park. It would be the seventh death in three years. It was always the same, two a year. A woman would go missing then either not show up or be found at the bottom of one of the many craggy cliffs. Each one had been treated as an accident. And even though the reports stated no foul play, she had her doubts. As she pulled off the park loop road at the base of Mount Champlain, the sixth tallest mountain in the park, her fear swelled at the sight of three other blue-and-white cruisers, a couple of park ranger SUVs, and Maine Warden Service trucks.

Reality was, no one should have been out here. The infamous, precipice trail was closed between March 15 and August 15. It was something to do with peregrine falcons nesting. Which meant few people would have been using the trail.

One of the officers called out to her, “Over here,” and waved her over to the base. Dakota continued driving past an ambulance. She could hear the sound of a chopper in the distance. Often people who had been injured would be airlifted from the YMCA in Eden Falls to the medical center in Bangor. It wasn’t an easy task getting people off the island.

When she pushed open her door and stepped out into the heat of the day, she wished she hadn’t put a jacket on. A warm breeze coming off the ocean brushed against her skin. Thankfully the place wasn’t swarming with tourists. While the population on the island was only ten thousand, it received over 2.4 million visitors every year. Mostly hikers and campers looking to take in the sights, smells, and sounds of Maine.

Dakota ducked under a police barrier tape cordoning off the area, gave a curt nod to a few of the other cops. There weren’t many of them, eleven on the island and the chief of course. More often than not the park rangers and game wardens handled any deaths or searches for missing people in the park. Usually a search party would go out for five days, with tracking dogs and a helicopter. It was never easy, even worse if it occurred in the dead of winter. Quite often they had to call off the search due to bad weather.

As she got closer to the exposed cliffs with fixed iron rungs hammered into the granite, she could see the chief standing at the foot of the mountain, talking to Ted Bishop who was a game warden. Chief Kurt Danvers looked as if he had been stitched into his uniform. He was a large man with a pockmarked face. It was rare that she saw him wearing anything casual. A couple of paramedics were standing by waiting to take the body away.

She was dead, otherwise she would have been gone by now.

With such a small town to police, there were no detectives so to speak on the island. Dakota was the closest that they had to a detective. A few months ago she'd been away for several weeks of training but it was a far cry from the time that was required to become a fully fledged D.I. The budget in the town just didn't extend for it and of course there really hadn't been a need. They mainly dealt in domestic disputes while the Maine Warden Service and park rangers handled everything inside of the park.

"Hey Ted, who we got?" Dakota asked him.

"Female. Rachael Taylor." He flashed a driver's license. Dakota glanced at it. "Student from the University of Maine. Seems she was down here with a friend of hers but we haven't been able to locate her. Their belongings are still at Blackwoods Campground."

"How long's she been missing?"

"Less than forty-eight hours."

"Anyone notified the family yet?" Dakota asked.

"Not yet."

"Who reported it?"

"Dougy." Douglas Adams was a park ranger who was a little slow but it hadn't prevented him from doing his duties. He'd grown up in Eden Falls and was someone Ted had taken under his wing. He had wanted to be a game warden but hadn't passed the hiring process due to selling drugs. It was an immediate disqualifier. Somehow Ted had managed to put in a good word with a buddy of his and lo-and-behold, Dougy was now one of eighty full-time rangers in the off-season. That number rose to two hundred and fifty in-season. Yet with all the rangers patrolling the park, people were still going missing. Some of them were never found, the others showed up at the bottom of cliffs and below bridges.

"Hey Dougy, get your ass over here," Ted said.

Dakota crouched and looked over the body. Unlike some of the past deaths, the last three women had the same ligature marks on the ankles and hands. The Taylor girl was showing signs of deep knife wounds and hemorrhaging around the throat. Her body was partially stiff. Stiffness in the body usually dissipated somewhere between twenty-four to forty-eight hours. She took out some Vicks from her pocket and dabbed a couple of times under her nostrils. The air was heavy with the smell of rotting meat.

"She didn't die here."

"What?" Chief Danvers asked.

Dakota leaned in and pointed to the areas of her body where the blood had pooled. It was dark purple and black. "Look. You see the unnatural color of the skin here. It indicates she was moved here."

"But she has injuries which appear consistent with having landed against the rocks."

Dakota stood up, her eyes still on the body. "Of course she was dropped, but that wasn't what I think killed her."

She got nearer to her face.

"You see the hemorrhaging around the throat." She pointed. "She was strangled."

The chief stepped in and placed his hand on Dakota's shoulder, leading her off to one side. He spoke in a hushed voice. "Now, let's not jump to conclusions here, Woods. For all we know this might have been some kinky sex game that she was playing with her lover."

"Erotic asphyxiation?"

"Right. You know how these university types are."

Dakota shook her head and stifled a chuckle.

"No, I mean. She's young. Experimental and so forth." He paused, staring at her. "I'm saying we don't want to start turning this into something that it's not. We are in the middle of tourist season and if it gets out we have a killer on the loose, people are going to panic. Then I'm going to have the town manager on my case. You know how these things go."

"You said the same thing with the Phelps girl."

Elisa Phelps had gone missing the previous year. Her body was found washed up on the shore.

"No. The coroner's office determined the cause of death was erotic asphyxiation."

"Two young university students die from the same thing in a span of a year. Both of them found in the vicinity of Acadia's mountains and this one is showing signs of knife wounds. Now I'm not an expert, especially since I was pulled out of D.I. training, but I'm pretty certain these deaths are connected."

Danvers threw a hand up while the other rested on his

utility belt. "Now you are jumping the gun." His brow knit together before he gestured to two officers to go and make sure the media didn't get through. An excited crowd of people had begun to gather by the entrance.

"So what do you want to do?"

"Let the coroner perform the exam. We'll go from there."

"What about the media?"

"Let's not release anything yet."

Dakota blew out her cheeks. She saw Dougy stepping a little too close to the body.

"Hey Dougy, don't go messing up my crime scene," she said.

"Crime? Go get a coffee or something, Woods. We'll deal with this."

"And the families?"

"I'll have one of the officers notify them."

"How am I meant to investigate if you keep stopping me from doing my job?"

"Woods, you're a fine officer but a lousy investigator."

She couldn't believe he had the nerve to say it. Then again the whole department still had a very old boys' club mentality. She had to fight her way into the position she held. It hadn't come without a fair amount of pushing and shoving. She put up a finger and tapped the air as she turned to walk away. "Then maybe you should have let me finish my training."

He muttered something to do with cutbacks and the town manager making the call on what they could or couldn't do. It was all political nonsense. Anyone would think the entire town was under the thumb of Wes Perkins.

"Hey, Woods. Call over to the university and see what you can dig up on her," he said.

She rolled her eyes. Like she hadn't thought of that.

From there she took a drive over to Blackwoods Campground. It was located just off Route 3 near Blackwoods Road and Otter Cove. A large brown sign made it clear to campers that there was no more room. It was always full. You had to book months in advance. As she drove up to the registration building, she glanced at a young family walking back from the beach. With towels tossed over their shoulders and the father holding his small child's hand, they looked as if they were enjoying their vacation.

Danvers was right. They had to be careful. Tourists brought in a large chunk of the island's income. A loss of revenue in the summer months could really damage businesses.

The registration building was a small house made from clapboard. A large American flag flapped around in the wind. A lone patrol car was parked outside.

Chapter 6

On Saturday mornings they began at nine. At least they were meant to. Ben had called up to Chloe four times to get out of bed. It had become a routine. Thirty minutes of sparring out in the yard. Ben would wear the boxing pads, Chloe would slip on sparring gloves and go toe to toe with her old man.

Chloe leaned out of the window with a white duvet wrapped around her. “Do we have to do this today?”

He smiled thinking she resembled a turtle.

“Do I have to answer that?”

She huffed and disappeared. A moment later, she appeared wearing gray sweats and a white shirt. “I swear you are the only father I know that makes his kid fight on weekends. Now I could understand it if I wanted to go into mixed martial arts but I don’t. Can’t we for once just have a normal Saturday?”

“Normal?”

"Yeah, you know, waking up at ten, crawling out of bed and spending half the day in my pajamas, breakfast at two, and alternating between watching goofy videos online and movies until midnight."

"What and waste all of this?"

Ben spun around with his arms open, smelling the morning air. It was a crisp blue sky, not a cloud in sight. The Weather Channel said that the temperatures were meant to hover in the high seventies. He stood waiting for her in a small clearing between the trees. A few sailboats were already moving out of the bay for the day.

"Okay, put 'em up."

"Really, this is getting old, Dad."

"You need to stay ready for nut jobs like the guy who tried to put the moves on you yesterday."

She circled him feigning jabs, and then hit the pads with a right hook, followed by a left uppercut. For the past two years they had been doing this. At first it was out of fear; a father's natural instinct to protect his daughter. He knew he couldn't watch her twenty-four hours a day, but at least if she could fend off an attacker, that would give him some peace of mind. He'd often wondered if Henri's victims had attempted to fight back?

If ever there was a time for women to know how to protect themselves, it was in this day and age. Yesterday had only confirmed that. Despite his anger at her for playing hooky, he was pleased to see that she had fought back. Whether she could have got out of the situation was another thing entirely. That's why he continued to hammer home the need for her to be on her guard. Sure, she was at an age where she was growing tired of it. But the truth was, it was another way to bond with his daughter. It wouldn't be long before she was off to college.

"Remember to use a kick if an opening presents itself."

A few seconds after, she winded him with a kick to the side.

"What, like that?" She gave a smirk.

"Alright, smart-ass."

They continued for another twenty minutes until the

front doorbell rang.

"I'll get that," Chloe said.

"No, keep practicing, you need it."

He chuckled, tossing the pads on the grass and jogging into the house. He was wearing a navy blue hoody with the FBI Academy logo on the breast, gray sweat pants, and sneakers. His white T-shirt below it was soaked through with sweat. On his way to the door he snatched up a bottle of ice-cold water.

Chapter 7

The man pulled off the thick, disfigured latex mask that made him look like an old man. It was chilling to look at but all part of hiding his identity. It also scared the living shit out of them. He entered a room with hewed stone walls.

It was damp down there but a perfect spot for holding them. No one could hear their cries. He'd made certain of that.

He moved over to a table with a large mirror, five bright orange bulbs above it, and a makeup box. Two more latex masks were on the side. He turned on some music; something that would make his pulse race. Film scores. It got him excited and… he paused for a second then glanced at the mask.

That bitch! She had torn at his mask as she tried to escape.

He let out a guttural scream, slamming his fists against

the table. Rage filled him as he thought of how she had rejected his advances. Oh, how he made her pay for that. His chest rose and fell fast. In the background the sound of whimpering could be heard echoing. He turned his head ever so slightly and breathed in deeply, savoring the sound of their pitiful cries.

"Please, I want to go home."

Did they really expect him to let them go?

This was the best part. He staggered out of the room and made his way down to the solitary confinement. It was their own personal prison. What were they complaining about? They got fed twice a day, showered, had plenty of books to read and a real bed to sleep in. After putting the mask back on, he slid open the metal latch on the door and peered inside. The sight of him gawking at her made her cringe and cower against the wall. That's right. That's the way he wanted them to be. Afraid.

"I want to go home, please."

"Why would you? You are home," he muttered while

silently laughing to himself. Tears streamed down the girl's face. Most of them were like that. Compliant and willing to do whatever it took to get out. But they weren't ever getting out of here.

Behind him a voice shouted profanities.

"Let me out, you bastard. I will fucking end your life."

The sound of her beating on the door was delightful. Oh, he loved to break them down and chip away at their tough exterior. Those were the ones he loved the most. He walked over to the door and matched her banging kick for kick. He screamed like a lunatic.

"Let me out, I want to see my daddy and mommy. Boo fucking hoo," he let out a maniacal laugh mocking her.

"Come in here and I will tear you apart," she screamed.

He chuckled to himself. So brave and foolish. Those were the best. Oh they thought they were tough. If she was lucky, he would tear her apart and she would feel every moment of it. He opened the shutter to see this university sweetheart. Blonde and twenty-two years of age, she was a perky one. She ran at the door and spat a huge glob against his face. He smiled beneath his mask, wiped the spit from it, and licked it in front of her. Her face twisted in disgust. She tasted sweet, but she wasn't ready yet. A few more days. Like plucking a fruit before its time. It needed to ripen. If you tasted it too early, it would be bitter and hard. Too late and there was no resistance. And he loved the resistance that was all part of the fun. Watching the struggle and fight evaporate before squeezing out the light from their eyes was magical.

Chapter 8

Elizabeth's mother Janice waltzed in without being invited. Not that he minded. She was a good woman, strong, much like Elizabeth. She understood loss after having lost her own husband six years ago to cancer.

"Please tell me you are not still doing those sparring sessions."

"And good morning to you," Ben said with a smirk on his face. He took a swig from his water bottle then wiped a few beads of sweat from his brow. Janice went into the kitchen and waved to Chloe who was still punching and kicking the air. For someone that was around a hundred and twenty pounds she sure had one hell of a kick on her. Chloe looked like her mother. She had the same smile, green eyes, dark wavy hair, and the one-liner comebacks.

"Have you seen all the police out on the loop road?" she asked.

Ben set his drink down. He was half listening and

studying Chloe's punches.

"Ben."

"Right, police, yeah. What was that?"

She groaned. "There are several cruisers blocking the road. A few others were pulling people over, checking tires and asking questions about if anyone had seen anything suspicious in the last forty-eight hours. Have you heard of anything?"

Now anyone else might have shrugged it off and not given it a passing thought. Ben's mind went into overdrive. He moved into the living area and flicked on the TV. On a side table a photo frame had an image of the family together in better days. A few channels later he landed on Eden Falls News. A woman reporter stood just beyond yellow police tape reporting an accident that had occurred in the forest. Ben recognized the area behind her as the entrance to the precipice trail.

"We will update you as police release more information."

Ben flicked away through a few more channels and

then turned it off.

"I should probably go over and see what's going on."

Janice lightly placed her hand on his arm. "Ben, it's okay."

He ran a hand across his stubbled jaw. Right then, Chloe came into the room still wearing her mitts. "Everything okay?"

She could tell she had interrupted something.

"Yeah, yeah. It's fine. Come on, let's finish off."

That morning Janice cooked up a breakfast. Bacon, eggs, and French toast while Ben and Chloe finished off their sparring session. She was getting better every week. When they first arrived in Eden Falls, they sparred every few days. Beyond giving him peace of mind, it had become a great way to get his mind off the loss of Elizabeth and Adam.

Initially he had Chloe going alone to see Dr. Emily Rose. A way to get her talking again as she had stopped playing guitar and even talking. It took a few months but it worked. In fact, it worked so well that Dr. Rose suggested that perhaps Ben should arrange to see her, too. Of course he'd been against the idea. He'd always considered talking to someone about his feelings was a sign of weakness. It stemmed from his military days and seeped over into his time as a detective in Manhattan. By the time he made it into the FBI they were lucky if they could get him to open up to anyone except Elizabeth. She had a natural way of drawing it out of him.

Anyway, she eventually convinced him after Chloe got on his case.

She's nice, Dad, it actually helps, she would say.

The first meeting with her was full of awkward silence. The only noise came from the ticking clock and Ben clearing his throat every ten minutes. She said it was normal. In fact, it was part of the opening process. Words were only to be used when he was ready. So those first three months were spent saying very little. Eventually conversation moved to simple everyday events. More about Dr. Rose's life than his. Though in time that changed and she would ask how he was coping with

Chloe, and what he'd planned to do now that he wasn't actively in the field as an agent.

Therapy worked, but it was tough.

Chapter 9

Later that afternoon, Ben dropped off Chloe at her grandmother's. She was going to be staying there for the weekend. Janice said it was to help out, but really she just loved seeing her granddaughter. From there he headed down to Eden Harbor with Jinx. She would sit up front in the truck and stick her snout out the window, letting the breeze blow her lips around.

Eden Falls was nestled between the glacial lakes and mountains of Acadia and the rugged coast of the Atlantic Ocean. It had a small-coastal town charm that drew in millions of visitors from all over the United States. He pulled out onto Route 3, a narrow two-lane road that went down a steep winding hill until he could see the rocky coastline. Among the fish draggers who were offloading their catch and taking on new supplies, the harbor was packed with schooners, yachts, whale-watching tour boats, and even a visiting cruise ship that could be seen in the distance.

Main Street and the marina were the heart of the town. It was full of all your typical shops, restaurants, taverns, hotels, as well as bed and breakfasts. Busy and bustling with activity, there were around ten different roads that went downhill to the edge of the harbor. Dotted around the coastline were historic homes, mansions, and Victorian cottages.

He parked the truck on a steep incline right outside Calyn's Café. He kept the windows rolled down for Jinx and went to grab a bite to eat. He never worried about her. She usually curled up in a ball and went to sleep or watched the boats as they came in. There had only been a few times Ben had to come out and quiet her after she got overly excited from a group of seagulls that landed nearby.

The town had grown on Ben. At first he was used to living in Florida where the weather was warm all year round. But he liked the change of pace, the different seasons, and the locals were friendly. It was a quaint little place with old-fashioned lampposts, benches, and carved signs that blew back and forth in the wind. Most of the buildings were made from clapboard.

Calyn's had become a regular spot that he felt comfortable hanging out in. It wasn't a seedy bar, or a greasy spoon diner but a laid-back café with big lobster claws sticking out the front. Wyatt Calyn owned the place. He went in and took a seat by the window. Somewhere he could keep a close eye on Jinx.

The waitress came over with a pot of coffee; she poured it and asked if Ben wanted the usual. Two small lobster rolls and fries. They had so much on the menu but he always picked the same thing.

"Hey Ben," she said.

"Claire."

She had deep red hair that was tied back and wore a blue and white outfit that clung to her curvy body.

"Looks like we might be in for a storm."

He glanced out. "There's not a cloud in sight. What makes you think that?"

"I can taste it."

He couldn't help but grin. "What is that, an East Coast joke?"

"No, my papa used to say you could tell when a storm was coming, obviously by the odor in the air but there is also a sweet, pungent taste."

"Okay, if you say so."

She smirked and gave him a playful slap on the arm. "You want coleslaw with those fries?"

"No, I'm on a diet."

He always said that, and she always brought over the coleslaw. Inside the restaurant were three families—locals he'd seen around town. Calyn's was a little off the beaten path. Townsfolk mostly frequented it.

He glanced up at the silent TV. "You heard anything about what the police are doing, Calyn?"

Wyatt Calyn was about forty years of age. Short ginger hair but built like he had just stepped out of a muscle building contest. He usually wore a tight black T-shirt with the blue logo of his business in the left corner.

"Another accident."

"Did the news say that?"

"No, Patty, one of the staff, lives up that way. She asked one of the police on the way in today."

The door opened, a shrill of a bell rang out. Ben didn't pay any attention as he was too busy trying to figure out what the reporter on the TV was saying. They had the volume turned down.

"Hey Forrester," a gruff voice said. He knew immediately who it was. It was Jake Ashton's father. Wyatt obviously could tell by the way Earl Ashton was carrying himself that he was looking to kick off.

"Earl."

"Stay out of it, Wyatt."

"I'll toss you out on your ear if you start any trouble," Wyatt said.

"No trouble. I just want a word with him."

Ben turned slightly.

"Let's go, Forrester, outside."

"I'm just about to have my lobster lunch."

He leaned in. “I don’t care. I want a word with you.”

“Whatever you need to say, you can say it here.”

“I want an apology. For what your daughter did to my son.”

Ben laughed. “He got off lightly.”

“What?” Earl stammered.

“You heard me. If anyone should be apologizing, it’s him. But I’m guessing he left out the part about trying to rape my daughter.”

“That doesn’t give you or her the right to lay a hand on him. Now outside.”

“Earl, don’t make me come over there,” Wyatt gave him another warning.

Meanwhile Claire returned with Ben’s lunch. She placed it on the table in front of him then walked away. Earl leaned in, picked up one of the lobster rolls and dropped it into Ben’s coffee.

“Oh I wish you hadn’t done that. I really like my lobster.”

“You need to keep that bitch of yours in line. You hear

me?"

"C'mon, don't say that. Just take a seat, Earl."

Ben was about to take the next lobster roll when Earl pushed the entire plate onto the floor.

"What are you going to do about it?"

Ben felt his jaw clench. He was trying his hardest not to lose his cool but this guy was really pushing his buttons. "If you've got a problem with the way it went down, take it up with the police."

"We already have. And they aren't doing a goddamn thing about it. Now Jake said you laid a hand on him."

Ben turned in his seat. "To get him off my daughter."

"That doesn't give you the right to touch another man's son."

"I think you are overlooking the fact your son forced himself on her."

"Maybe your daughter asked for it. Have you thought about that?" He prodded Ben's arm. "Now you listen here."

"Just back off." Ben slapped his hand away.

"Oh you wanna touch me?"

Right then he grabbed a handful of Ben's shirt and pulled up. It was the stupidest thing he could have done. Ben stood up fast, wrapped his arm over Earl's, and pushed upwards forcing his elbow up. He slapped him twice in the throat with the side of his hand and knocked him onto another table. All chaos broke loose. Wyatt hopped over the bar, Ben backed up with his arms up. Dakota Woods came in the door. Before Earl could react, she stepped in the middle.

Gripping his own throat and giving the worst performance of his life Earl choked out the words, "I want to press charges against this man."

"Go walk it off, Earl. I saw everything," Wyatt said.

Dakota cast a glance at Ben who was picking up the plate.

"No need. I can do that," Claire said, coming along with a dustpan and broom.

Earl couldn't believe it. He scowled at Ben, brushed himself off and was seen to the door by Dakota.

Chapter 10

Ben learned a few more things about the town that day. They tended to deal with their own disputes quietly. It wasn't that the police looked the other way; in fact, it was quite the opposite. They were quick to nip things in the bud.

"Sorry about that, Wyatt," Ben said.

Wyatt tossed a cloth over his shoulder. "Don't worry, but listen, you might want to dial it back, people around here talk."

Ben cast a glance around the room. A few murmurs came from the other patrons.

"We'll get you another plate of food."

"You know what, I think I've lost my appetite."

Wyatt looked pissed. Ben thought it was because some of the people at the other tables had got up and left. He tossed a few more dollars on the table. "That's to pay for the plate."

He waved him off. “Hey you don’t need to, Earl smashed it.”

“It doesn’t matter.”

As Ben was about to leave, Dakota approached him.

“Got a minute?” she asked.

“If you want to tag along. I was just leaving.”

He stepped outside and saw that Earl was gone.

“I guess he’ll be filing charges over that?”

“No, Wyatt said he saw what happened. That’s good enough for me. But I am curious, did they teach you that move in the FBI?”

“Not exactly.”

They walked down to the town pier and started walking along the Shore Path that was located in front of Eden Harbor Inn. To the right was Agamont Park where people converged to soak in the atmosphere. Off in the distance he could see a landmass east of the bay called Bar Island. When there was a low tide a natural bridge between Eden Falls and the island could be seen and used to get to the island. Chloe had taken him out there once.

“What’s going on in Acadia Park?” Ben asked

“That’s what I wanted to talk you about.”

They passed a water fountain. The steady flow of water created ripples on the surface that fanned out to the stone edges. A few fishermen shouted to one another from their boats.

“A girl is dead and one is missing.”

“How old?”

“Twenty-two, she’s from Bangor. Studying at the University of Maine.”

“That explains the chopper in the air.”

A few people were out walking their dogs, another couple jogging. Dakota gave them a nod.

“Any leads on the missing girl?”

“None so far. In fact, they are liable to sweep this all under the rug.”

“How so?”

She momentarily stopped near a waist-high, black steel fence before continuing to walk.

“Over the past three years we have had seven deaths.

Two women every summer."

"That's not a lot for a national park."

"It is around here. The last death we had dates back to twenty-two years ago," she replied.

He glanced at her but didn't say anything.

"Anyway, usually people show up, or the rescue team finds them, but these women are different."

"In what way?"

"All of them are young, in their early twenties. Usually from a university."

"Are they always together when they go missing?"

"No. Not until these last two went missing. The previous victims weren't connected. Last year one was a hiker on a day trip, the other was camping. But all of them lived off the island."

"So he chooses women from outside the area."

"He?"

"Well, I'm guessing all of them were raped?"

"Raped, strangled, and dumped. Except the first five. They weren't strangled but there were vaginal and anal tears consistent with a brutal rape. The first five were found in various places around Acadia and all of them close to a cliff."

"And where do I come into the picture?" he asked.

"I was wondering if you could look over the files. Maybe give your opinion on them?"

"I don't do that anymore."

She stopped walking. "I thought you were with the FBI?"

"On paper, yeah, but it's been two years since I was in the field."

"But you're still teaching."

This time it was him who stopped. "How do you know that?"

"I dug around. Asked a few questions." She smiled. "Don't worry, it's nothing that I wouldn't have done with anyone else."

"And I'm meant to believe that?"

They continued walking.

"Anyway. I was wondering…"

"Not to be rude, Officer Woods–"

"Dakota. Just call me Dakota."

He cleared his throat and looked out at the blue ocean. Frothy waves crashed against the big rocks with deadly force. The wind was picking up. Maybe Claire was right. Perhaps a storm was on its way.

"You don't know anything about me."

Dakota stepped a little closer. "Six foot two, two hundred pounds, forty-one years of age, you did four years in the U.S. Army, and seven as a homicide detective in New York before joining the FBI. You have a bachelor's degree in sociology and physical education. A master's of science in psychology and a PhD in classifying homicides. You served on the FBI SWAT team as a sniper, then later as a hostage negotiator. You were transferred to the FBI behavioral sciences unit after seven years as a field agent and you taught hostage negotiation, forensics, and criminal psychology at the FBI Academy in Quantico." She took a breath and continued. "You teach online lectures in analysis, interviewing, and assessing human and group behavior, you have a daughter that is seventeen, and you were recently widowed and lost a son. My condolences."

He nodded his head, slowly studying her face.

"Then you'll understand why I can't be involved."

"I'm not asking you to get involved, just a little help."

"Dakota. I admire all the effort digging into my past but that doesn't mean you know me."

"Does it matter? I'm talking about a young girl's life that could be in jeopardy. Look, I know you caught seven other serial killers."

"Six, the last one got away." His eyes dropped.

Dakota breathed in deeply. "Dr. Forrester."

"Ben."

"Right. Ben, I just know that you think differently than most around here, and I could use your insights. Besides, if this person isn't caught, they are going to keep on doing it. All I'm asking is for you to look over the reports and let me know what you think."

She handed him a thin brown leather folder that was

zipped up. Ben glanced at it.

"I can't promise anything."

She tilted her head. "No, I understand."

As they retraced their way back Ben spoke, "Only one thing."

"What's that?"

"You owe me a beer after this."

"Done."

They continued walking.

"One thing you forgot to mention in your analysis of me."

"What's that?" she asked.

"Boxers or briefs?"

She snorted. "That's too easy. Briefs. You're definitely a briefs man."

He smiled.

Chapter 11

He stared at the folder, tapping his fingers against the side table. He got up and poured himself a scotch on the rocks and downed it. It was the middle of the afternoon and he'd already contacted a local security firm to come and install a security alarm system with twenty-four-seven monitoring. Whether this was a killer or Dakota's wild imagination, he wasn't going to take any chances. How had this slipped by him? He couldn't remember the police blocking off the roads in the past two years or any reports of deaths in the park.

In the first six months of arriving in Eden Falls, he'd checked daily for information on missing people — then again, come to think of it, he'd always focused on locations closer to the Everglades.

He sipped his drink and let the warmth wash over him. He felt his muscles unwind as he kicked his shoes off and looked out over the bay.

Over the course of two hours he puttered around the house and kept his mind occupied on anything else except that folder. He knew why he didn't want to open it. He'd seen countless bodies. It wasn't the macabre that intrigued him, it was an interest in criminology.

His cell phone buzzed and rattled against the wood table. He went over and answered it. It was Nate Mueller.

"Nate."

"Ben, how are you?"

He could hear the sound of agents in the background punching keys and talking on the phone. He was calling from his office. It was always his office. That's because Nate was a workaholic just like Ben had been. It was one of the many reasons why they got on so well; that, and of course because they went through the academy together. They were driven, Nate would say. Driven to catch predators. It was true. The cases got under his skin. That's why he hadn't opened that folder. The need to solve crime drove both of them to work long hours even when others had clocked out. There was no off switch for them.

Once they got involved in a case they lived and breathed it every waking moment. It became their world.

The Skinner case had almost destroyed him. He wasn't sure he wanted to face that again. It had taken the better part of two years to lay it to rest. *Lay it to rest?* What a joke. He hadn't laid it to rest. It lingered there in the back of his mind, taunting him like an unseen ghost. Beckoning him to spend the rest of his life chasing someone who would probably never show his face again. And that was it. He didn't even know what Henri Bruns looked like or if that was his real name. He'd been smart. Played his cards well and had an exit strategy.

"I'm still alive," Ben replied as usual.

"How's Chloe?"

"As good as can be."

"I was going to come out there but you know how it is…"

"You doing okay?" Ben asked. He was worried about the mental state of his friend. He'd seen so many agents commit suicide. It wasn't uncommon in law enforcement.

Stress, suicide, alcohol abuse, and marital discord were just a few of the things that plagued agents. Though the suicide rate was lower in the FBI than in other areas of law enforcement, it still occurred. Some couldn't handle what they saw. For others it was personal issues.

"We could really use your insights out here, Ben."

"Nate, you have more than enough agents."

"But not ones that think like you."

"That's why they're trained by me remotely."

"You can't learn this stuff, Ben. You should know that. It's a gut instinct. Some have it, some don't."

"I think you're mistaken. If I had it, he'd be sitting on death row right now."

Nate must have put the phone up to his chest as his voice became muffled. "You want to keep it down?" he shouted to a group who were chatting in the background.

"Sorry about that. Where were we?"

Ben took another sip of his drink. "Something about placing me on a pedestal."

He laughed. "Hey, I heard you have a missing girl out

there?"

"Something like that."

"Oh, you telling me you aren't looking into it?"

Ben glanced at the folder on the side table.

"Nate, I'm out of it."

He snorted on the other end of the line. "Guys like you and me are never out of it. It's in our blood. It's what we do."

"Not anymore."

Ben had been placed on administrative leave pending reassignment after the death of his family. It was only meant to be six months. That turned into a year, then two. At first it was paid leave, then Ben wasn't sure if he wanted to go back. The FBI wasn't sure they wanted to lose him so it was agreed that he would be placed on unpaid leave until he felt ready to return. In the meantime he agreed to provide remote training as and when needed. It wasn't the best situation but for him it worked.

"Any leads on Bruns?" Ben asked.

"No, the guy's a ghost."

"I mean deaths that match his M.O.?"

"There's been a few but nothing that we can link for sure to him. Right now they've got us working the case of someone who is killing people and drinking their blood."

"Lovely," Ben replied sarcastically.

"Yeah and that's not the half of it. If the public knew what he was doing there would be mass panic."

Besides the obvious reasons of wanting to spare the public unneeded agony and fear, quite often certain facts that only the killer would know would be withheld. Later, when interrogating a suspect, those facts could prove to be very useful. It was the reason why no one knew about what Skinner had done with his victim's bodies. The public wasn't told about those details. He'd wondered what people would have thought if they had known that the exhibit was found to contain skinned murdered victims.

Instead agents were the ones who had to carry those grisly details around with them in their head. It was the stuff of nightmares. They got to see the underbelly of the world and take it home.

"You have any leads on the guy?" Ben asked.

"Yeah, we've developed a profile of him. Disorganized, young, thin probably living within a mile radius of the killings."

It wasn't a guarantee that profiling would lead to the capture, but it definitely narrowed the search and often was accurate. It made searching a little easier. It gave the local police pounding the pavement someone to look for and it ruled out the nut jobs that would come forward claiming they had done the murders. It never ceased to amaze him how many innocent oddballs would turn themselves in just so they could claim the title of a serial killer and have their fifteen minutes of fame.

But that title wasn't anything to be proud about.

"Well, hey, I've got to go. Speak soon."

"Good to hear from you, Nate."

After hanging up he had to wonder if Nate called him out of need more than concern. For years they'd been a sounding board for each other. So much had changed. But that hadn't.

Ben glanced again at the folder, then picked it up and opened it.

Chapter 12

It was a media circus. It was believed the family had contacted them. The chief wanted to keep it all low-key and let the Maine Warden Service and search-and-rescue try to locate the other girl. But the parents weren't satisfied.

The missing girl was Helen Hayes, a resident of Ellsworth, Maine.

Ellsworth was a small city and the county seat of Hancock County situated on the mainland. It was a short drive but one that was filled with dread. It never got easy, but at least another officer had done the hard part. Every parent handled disappearances differently. Some would leap into action and be actively involved in the search party while others just went to pieces.

By the time Dakota drove up to the Hayes house on Chapel Street it was evening and the rain was hammering the windshield. Outside the local Ellsworth police had cordoned off the area and were trying to keep back a barrage of media and neighbors. Some of them were already pointing the finger at the police for not doing enough. The previous disappearances didn't get as much attention because the bodies were found within a matter of days and ruled an accident. It wasn't like the National Park Service wasn't forthright in letting the public know of the dangers of hiking in the mountains of Acadia. They made it clear with a big yellow caution sign that let hikers know that people had been injured and even died on the mountainsides.

Now if all the bodies had shown no sign of ligature marks, then maybe the public wouldn't have been so outraged. But Rachael Taylor and the Phelps girl were the first two to have been strangled. And Rachael, the first to show signs of knife wounds.

Dakota pulled up and flashed her badge to one of the officers outside. She parked just beyond the house. Chief Danvers was already on scene along with state police. Dakota glanced back at the mob that was gathered outside and shook her head. Had they called in the FBI after the third death, perhaps the other girls could have been spared a similar fate.

Inside the home it wasn't much better. The moment the chief caught sight of Dakota he came over.

"This is spiraling out of control real fast. Do you know who leaked this to the media?"

"The family."

He shook his head, exasperated.

"Where are they?"

"Through there but just be careful what you say. The father is already irate as it is."

"By the way, did they get any fibers, prints, or DNA from the body of the Taylor girl?" Dakota asked.

"Nothing. Clean as a whistle."

Danvers led the way. Inside it was a typical home. Nothing fancy. Hardwood floors, a two-story, three-bedroom home. The Hayes family had two children. Inside the living room was a black upright piano, two couches, and a fireplace.

“Is this the FBI?” the father immediately blurted out.

“No, I’m Detective Woods, well, Officer Woods but I'm kind of in between training.”

She glanced at Danvers who shook his head.

“Please tell me you have got an idea where our baby is?”

She took a deep breath. There was only one thing worse than telling a family that their son or daughter was dead. It was telling them you had no idea where they were.

“We are looking into it. Is there anyone that you know who might have wanted to harm Helen?”

The father blew out his cheeks and went over to the fireplace. Helen’s mother, who was perched on the edge of the couch, her eyes red from crying, spoke. “No, she kept to herself. A good kid. She was really looking forward to graduating from college and becoming a marine biologist.”

“What about friends?”

“Other than Rachael, there were a couple of other girls

but we have already called their homes and she's not there."

"You don't think she would have run away?"

The very mention of it sent the father into a rage. "Oh no, you are not going to try to spin this around. She has a good home. Good grades. There's nothing that would give her reason to run. Someone has taken her."

"We're not exactly sure about that right now, Mr. Hayes. Um, so this camping trip, what do you know about it?"

The mother dabbed the corner of her eyes with a tissue before replying. "It was to be a four-day getaway. I don't understand it. Blackwoods Campground gets campers all the time. It's safe. There are lots of people there. How could she go missing?"

"Acadia is massive," the chief said. He wasn't kidding. It had twenty-six glacier-carved mountain peaks. The forest which covered over 42,000 acres was full of lakes and ponds and over 120 miles of trails. The terrain of rugged shorelines, deep woods, and open mountain summits could be treacherous even to the savviest hikers. Then if the weather was bad, search parties were called off in a matter of days and people would never be seen again. That's what made it the perfect hunting ground for a predator. Add to that, frequent disappearances in national parks all across the United States and it was rare for anyone to jump to the conclusion that a serial killer was behind them. It was usually notched up as animals, or hiker's error.

"You have my word, Mr. and Mrs. Hayes. We will find her and catch whoever did this," she said.

"Excuse us," Danvers raised a finger. "We'll be right back."

Danvers did his best job to strong-arm Dakota out of the room without making it look like he was bothered by what she'd said. Outside he closed the doors behind him.

He immediately got right up in her face. "What are you doing?"

"What's the problem?"

"You go telling them that someone is behind the

disappearance and state police and FBI will be all over this."

Dakota shook her head and scoffed. "And that's a problem? We could use all the help we can get."

"We already have enough people out there right now searching."

"You still think this is just a case of two people who got lost? People who go for a hike and turn up dead, Chief, don't have ligature marks around their neck or signs of being raped."

"People are into kinky sex nowadays. It doesn't mean anything."

Dakota put her hands on her hips and shook her head in disbelief. It wasn't that the chief was ignorant. He was juggling many hats in the town.

Danvers took a deep breath and cast a glance around him. "You know how many homicides we have dealt with in Eden Falls since I've been chief?"

"No, but I'm sure you're going to tell me."

"Two, and those were personal disputes. Now I fully

intend to keep it that way. The town manager likes it that way. Tourists like it that way. The National Park Service likes it that way. Until we have more details from the coroner this is not a homicide. I want it to be treated that way. It's a missing case. It's suspicious but just a missing case. I'm sure the Hayes girl will be found alive and we'll find out that this was all just a bad sex game that went wrong."

It was all about appearances. Keeping the stats low. Making the powers that be happy.

"You really think that's the case? What, you think the Hayes girl stabbed her friend in some weird sex game and then ran off? It's still murder no matter how you spin this."

"I'm not having this conversation with you. Go do your job."

With that he turned around and went back into the living room.

Chapter 13

He shifted his position in the thick oak tree, feeling his foot cramp up. He'd been crouched for the better part of an hour watching her move from one room to the next. The aroma of smoke coming from a neighbor's fire reached his nostrils. It was sweet and pungent. In June the evenings were warm, slightly humid but perfect for watching them. He was breaking the routine but with police all over the campgrounds the chance of snatching one of those lovelies was virtually impossible.

But he wasn't going to stop. He couldn't.

At ten o'clock in the evening, darkness wrapped itself around the small town of Eden Falls. It seeped into the narrow alleys and small streets where only a few porch lights glowed.

He had nestled himself into an oak a short distance from the house. That was the beauty of Acadia, it swallowed many of the homes, making it easy to watch them. So many times he'd been tempted to pluck a few from their beds but that was risky. The campgrounds and late-night hikers were so much easier. They were used to the sound of branches snapping and the rustle of animals. He often felt like an animal crouched in the darkness waiting for his prey.

Tracking them was as much a part of the sexual excitement that fueled his fantasy as was the moment he struck. Staying hidden, slipping through the trees unnoticed, even catching them skinny-dipping in the lake.

He breathed in deeply, letting the aroma of the forest fill his lungs. He shifted again, getting hard at the thought of hunting another. One was never enough. There was only so much exhilaration found in holding them captive and making them do whatever he wanted. It was never enough. It could be better. He could take longer watching them. He licked his lips and felt his mouth go dry gazing at her. He brought out his gleaming knife and rubbed his thumb over the edge sideways just to feel how sharp it was. He gripped the stun gun in his pocket for the third time just to be sure it was still there.

They always wanted to know why? Why them? Walking around with those tight shorts on in the summer. Some of them even had letters printed on the back of their ass. Why them? They were like a beacon, beckoning him to reach out and taste what lay beneath all those clothes.

He ran the tip of his tongue around the outside of his teeth then bit lightly down on his bottom lip, savoring the fantasy. He wasn't sure what he liked more — the fact that he got away with it, or the thrill of walking among the townsfolk without them knowing.

He knew freedom that few men would experience. Oh the thought had slipped through their minds, and some had even attempted to do what he had mastered but they were amateurs. And so were the police. The public gave the police too much credit. If they only knew how tied their hands were or how little they knew about catching predators, they wouldn't even phone for help.

God, this location was fantastic. The house was nestled deep into the heart of his hunting ground. There were no floodlights to stop him. Even if the girl screamed, it wouldn't matter. Who was going to hear her out here? The closest neighbor was a good distance away.

He wanted to take more, but he had to be careful. Two a year, that was it. Usually spaced out by a month. Sure, the last time it had gone wrong but that wasn't his fault. Anyway, now he could even it out. It was all a matter of timing. He was in no rush, especially since he loved it.

The girl came back into view, her dark flowing hair, her perky little breasts protruding beneath that summer top. A yellow lab followed her into the living room. That wasn't going to be a problem. He'd brought the steak doused with a little special seasoning to keep it quiet.

His eyes ran the full length of her legs as she curled up on a sofa. She was athletic and had been kissed by the sun just enough to give her skin a delicious buttery appearance. Every second he watched he wanted to take her. *Wait, just hold on a little longer and she will be yours,* he told himself. He'd seen her around town. She was the kind of girl that took care of herself. She wasn't like the others who flaunted themselves like sluts. Those bitches got what they deserved. This time he gripped the blade in his hand, feeling it cut into his skin just a little. The fine line between pain and pleasure, oh how he loved to rock back and forth between the two.

She lay down, bringing her feet up behind her as she read a book. He watched her toes dance around. The urge to bite them made his pulse race. Oh, he wasn't stupid, a female like that would never go for him outside of doing this. Sure, people respected him but that wasn't enough. He didn't want respect. He wanted to dominate them. And he did.

By day, he observed them like he had in school. Too big. Too thin. Too ugly. Too much makeup. Too arrogant. They had to be just right. Everything from the way their ass curved, to the thickness of their thighs. It wasn't just the coeds he took. No, occasionally there were those in their thirties and forties that caught his attention. He laughed silently at them as they tried to pretend they were in control. He watched them set up their tents, hike out into the forest, and give out advice as if they were God. But they weren't. He was. They just didn't know it yet.

Where was she? He'd taken his eyes off her for just a brief moment. His eyes frantically scanned the downstairs and upstairs. Every room was lit up, giving him a clear shot. *Where are you?* Then he heard the sliding door open. *Oh, there you are.* The lab bounded out, and she followed. He swallowed hard at the anticipation of taking her. The dog sniffed the air then looked in his direction. He didn't move an inch. There was no need. The darkness of the night and his black clothes and mask shrouded him. The only thing visible was his eyes. He brought his lids down to a slit. He didn't want the glow from the house to reflect or give away his position. He'd spent far too long building up to this.

"What's up, boy?"

The dog was barking up a storm. *Shut the hell up,* he thought. The tall, slender girl looked towards him, her eyes squinting.

"There's nothing there, silly dog. Come on in."

She turned and padded back into the house. The dog gave a deep growl then followed in her shadow. His eyes followed her back through the house as she went to the fridge and took out a bottle of milk. She poured herself a glass and downed it. A creamy white remained at the corners of her mouth, only exciting him more. As she turned to go back into the living room, she twisted her hair up and grabbed a wooden hairpin to hold it in place. She switched on the TV, grabbed a magazine off the side table and flipped through it. She sat in a large round wicker chair, opening and closing her legs as if she was clapping her knees. Did she know he was here? Was she baiting him to come and pluck her innocence? He was going to take his time with this one. Her death wasn't going to come fast. They would play first. Days of playing. He wanted to trace every inch of her body with his blade. The thought of teasing her nipples with the tip sent his mind into overdrive.

He was sick, he knew that. At least that's the way society saw him. But everyone was sick in their own way. They lived within the restraints, claiming they were free. They were slaves to a society that hedged them, gave them rules, and subtly shaped them from childhood into what they wanted. A polite and kind member of society. It was foolish.

He embraced his darkness. It was within every man and woman, but only a few stared down into the abyss. Even fewer dropped in. If they only knew what it was like in there. How good it felt to be liberated from the borders society had placed on them.

He had returned to his primal state. It was fierce and wild but every bit perfect.

The sound of gravel being chewed up caught his attention. His eyes darted to two beams of light flickering in the trees. It was getting closer. In the distance he could see the vehicle now.

He slipped the ten-inch serrated knife into its sheath and pulled back into darkness.

A door slammed closed, then voices. A jingle of keys and there was another figure moving through the house. He smiled, double the fun.

She was older, but he didn't have any preferences. Preferences got you profiled, and he wanted to keep them confused. He waited. He would bide his time and when all the lights went out, he would show them the true nature of a man.

His eyes fell on the girl again as she turned her head to greet the woman.

Wait for me. I'm coming. We'll soon be together.

Chapter 14

Ben awoke to a knock at the window. It had become part of his dream. His eyelids fluttered and a warm band of light covered his body as he lay back in the chair. He'd fallen asleep in the sunroom. Scattered over his body were photos of the crime scenes. Each snapshot, a corpse in a different stage of decomposition.

Beyond the window was Dakota. She was holding two cups of coffee, a smirk spread across her face as he registered where he was. He tilted his head from side to side and it let out a crack. His one arm felt weighted and dead as though all the blood had pooled in one area. He slipped out from under the blanket of photos, letting them slide to the floor, and shuffled over to the back door. Ben unlocked and pulled it open.

"Morning. Brought you a coffee. Not sure how you take it."

She handed it to him and walked in without even

asking.

"Please. Come in," he said.

The sunroom had heated floors and drew in natural light that kept it warm even though the temperature outside had dropped. In the sky, dark clouds threatened rain.

"You sleep out here often?" she asked, glancing around at the disarray.

"Yeah, when it strikes my fancy."

"Or when you've drunk a little?" she said, picking up an empty bottle of bourbon. He took it from her and tossed it into a wicker trashcan with two others.

"Are you here to judge me?"

"No, I was hoping to hear your thoughts on the reports I gave you… which… I can see you thoroughly went through."

She gazed at the mess of jumbled paperwork before picking it up and trying to figure out which report went with certain photos. Meanwhile, Ben exited to take a piss. After, he splashed some cold water on his face and gazed at the bags under his eyes. He pulled at them and took a closer look at his bloodshot eyes. He needed more sleep, but that wasn't going to happen. He ran the tip of his fingers through his dark hair in an attempt to smooth out the bedhead mess. Ben ran a hand over his stubbled chin, it was showing a good amount of gray at the front. Aging had once bothered him. Now he couldn't care less. It was a step closer to seeing Elizabeth.

When he returned, Dakota was looking at the photo of his family.

"If you don't mind, I'd prefer..."

Her eyebrow shot up. "Right. Sorry." She set it back down and took a seat. "She was a beautiful woman. Good-looking kid too."

"Yeah," he muttered under his breath. "How are you getting on with the missing girl?"

He shifted the topic away after getting a feeling she was about to dig deeper into his past. It wasn't that he wouldn't have shared it, but he had Emily and Nate for that. As it stood his slate was clean here. No one knew about him, or at least had mentioned his past involvement in the FBI until now. He wanted to keep it that way. There was something very comforting about anonymity. It was the reason he didn't want his face on books. He wasn't clamoring to be noticed. His success in the bureau wasn't all down to him but he knew that everything got viewed through that lens because of his involvement in nationwide cases. In the eyes of the media and public he was the guy whose profiles had caught killers. But this was not exactly true. The police were the ones who apprehended. Leads from citizens and a fair amount of luck played a large role. The profiles he created were just a tool. A means of filtering through the chaos and mess to pinpoint a cluster of individuals who might be responsible. He'd *helped* catch killers, nothing more.

"No leads. Search crews have turned up nothing and they are still out there."

"It's frustrating isn't it? How long have you been with the department, Woods?" He nursed his coffee, took the lid off and steam spiraled above it.

She gave him a look, and he remembered she wanted him to address her by her first name.

"Five years. Three of those were on patrol. I'm still a rookie in the chief's eyes."

It only required two years to be eligible to become a detective.

"How many others?"

"Just me. I mean, there are other officers, but I was the only one crazy enough to want to follow through and get trained." She paused. "And even then they pulled me out, halfway through training. But, hopefully, I will return in a few months to complete it."

"Why?"

"Small-town politics. Budget versus need. We don't exactly get a lot of homicides here."

"Considering the FBI?"

Her eyes locked on him. "Yeah… it's more of an aspiration than a solid goal. I'll probably complete my training and take a position with the state police or follow through with the FBI."

"Well, I'm sure my books will dissuade you."

"You say that like you hate it?"

"No. Just it can eat you up and spit you out."

She glanced again at the photo. He quickly moved on before she began questioning.

"Your perp is going to take another," Ben said before taking a sip of coffee.

Her brow pinched. "Why? He's already taken two this year," she said.

"One got away from him."

"But she was found dead?"

"That was after. Punishment. If you look at all the victims. She was the one that was stabbed. That's personal. He was enraged. It's just a hunch but I think she got away from him. Anyway, he'll take another because it's all part of his fantasy. It has to be perfect. That last one wasn't perfect. Far from it."

Ben flipped through the photos before handing it all to her.

"What about the others?" Ben asked.

"Those not found?"

"Yeah."

"Still classified as lost."

"Okay, so he keeps some of them alive. Search the National Park Service records for other disappearances where no one was found. I'm betting you'll find a similar match to these other girls. He hasn't taken seven, he's taken a lot more."

Dakota took a sip of her coffee and looked down at the photos.

"He's getting more reckless. Sloppy then?"

"No," he replied

"But she got away."

"Not because of a lack of oversight on his part. No, I think that was all her doing. She was smart. No, this guy is organized, methodical."

"What do you mean?"

"There are only two types of predators out there. The organized and disorganized. Based on what I've seen in the crime scene photos and reports, he stalks his victims.

Watches them for some time. He never left behind any trace evidence that might incriminate him. He's careful but vindictive if crossed. He's been doing this a while and he'll continue until he's caught."

She nodded and put her drink down.

"What makes you believe it's a male if no semen was found?"

"Sexual crimes are usually done by males in their twenties and thirties." He swallowed down the rest of his coffee. "You want some breakfast?"

Chapter 15

At fifteen minutes past nine, Ben was beginning to feel human again. A cheese omelet always hit the spot. He'd tossed back two Tylenol to fend off the throbbing in the back of his head and refilled Dakota's cup.

"Thanks."

She glanced up at him with those blue eyes that were kind of mesmerizing. He hadn't seen her out of uniform. He eyed her, making his way back to the breakfast table. She was short compared to him.

"So what about you?" Ben asked.

"Not much to say, really."

He took a seat across from her and bit down on his toast.

"Anyway, you're the expert. What can you tell me?" she enquired.

He stifled a laugh. "You were engaged or married for five years."

"Six actually."

"Yeah, I guess the white band on your finger is fading but could be the summer weather." He leaned back in his chair, taking in her five-foot-eight frame with long, strawberry blonde hair.

"You grew up around here. You've wanted to get out for years and that's why you have an interest in the FBI. This place doesn't challenge you."

"Is that why you think I came to you?" she asked.

He smirked. "If it is, I would hate to disappoint."

"What else?"

Dakota seemed to be enjoying this. Perhaps he would have continued if the case wasn't weighing heavily on his mind.

"Maybe another time."

That only made her smile. "This guy. You said he was organized, can you elaborate?"

Ben took a deep breath. "Contrary to what people might think, he's not schizophrenic or paranoid but calm and collected. You're dealing with someone who holds a position of power. He's comfortable in it. Has the respect of those around him but not women. He's not skinny, and he dresses well to blend in."

"Not skinny?"

"Despite what you might be thinking, he's in a good state of mind. All of this. Even the police showing up. It's nothing to him. He still thinks he's in control and he is. He sleeps well, eats well, and if you passed him on the street or spoke to him, you wouldn't even know it. He's more than likely had a string of relationships. Short-lived, uneventful… even forgettable."

She leaned forward, clasping her hands beneath her chin.

He continued, "Look for someone with a military background who was kicked out, someone who would have made a good recruit. Careful, organized and can follow rules but chooses not to."

"What about a job?" she asked.

"He has one. Something that lets him observe the comings and goings of his victims, and as for transportation... Whatever it is... you'll find it clean. Spotless even. He has a high attention to detail."

She set her knife and fork down and sat back in her chair with her coffee, studying him. "You got all of that from the reports and photos? You should consider joining the department."

He snorted. "Maybe in another lifetime."

She glanced around the room and then ran her hand around Jinx's face. "Where's Chloe?"

"At her grandmother's. You know Janice Turner?"

"Oh yeah, of course. I never knew that was your wife's mother."

"And after all that research on me?" he said playfully.

"Do you mind?" She wanted to look around.

"Go ahead."

He gathered up the plates and rinsed the remainders off then slotted them into the dishwasher. He could see her running her hands over the psychology books he had in his office.

"You read all of these?"

"Yep. Dry as heck, but insightful. You can borrow them if you like."

"I might do that."

In two years he hadn't had anyone over besides Janice. It's not that he couldn't have, he just didn't feel ready to open up to anyone new or surround himself with large groups of people. The times he ventured out to the grocery store he felt as though he was suffocating from the crowds. It just became easier to get it delivered. Not that he cooked much.

She strolled from room to room before returning.

"So what's on the agenda for today?" he asked.

"A press conference. They want to calm the public's fears."

"Good luck with that."

It rarely did any good. If anything, it had a tendency to infuriate people and get the public riled up. The police hated doing them; it only made them feel incompetent if they had nothing to offer beyond the generalized palatable version of what had happened. Essentially they regurgitated what the media already knew.

"Do you want to come with me to the crime scene?" she asked.

Ben leaned back against the kitchen counter and chewed on the inside of his cheek.

"Like maybe if you tagged along you might see something we've overlooked."

"Woods," he said.

"Dakota."

"Look, Woods, I don't think that would be a good idea."

He knew what Dr. Rose would have suggested. She would have encouraged him to go, and, maybe he should. It had been a while since he'd got his hands dirty with an investigation. But then the more he pondered it, he could feel his pulse beating a little faster. He swallowed hard. *Not now.* He turned to look for his migraine medication. He'd been getting them less frequently but since going over the reports and seeing dead bodies, it was starting again.

"I think I'll take a rain check. I'm not feeling too good and I…" he cleared his throat. "I have to pick up my daughter later."

"Sure, okay, just thought I would ask."

He wanted her to leave now but didn't want to be rude. Thankfully she must have picked up on it.

"Well, thanks for the breakfast and your insights. Hopefully we can catch this guy."

He nodded but didn't say anything. It had been a bad mistake looking over the reports. He wasn't ready to deal with it. A flood of memories bombarded his mind as he shook out a couple of pills and tossed them back with the remainder of his coffee.

An hour after she left he poured himself a small scotch. Just a little to take the edge off things. The phone rang, but he didn't answer it. A few seconds passed and then it rang again. He wasn't going to answer it, but he wanted to see who was calling. He looked at the caller ID. It was Janice.

He immediately picked up, expecting her to go into

her usual spiel about how he wasn't feeding Chloe enough greens or vitamins. Instead, what she said made him drop the phone.

Chapter 16

Four police cars, along with a game warden truck, were outside Janice's home. One of them was Dakota's. Ben tore into the driveway and jumped out, leaving the door on his vehicle open. An officer immediately stepped forward with his arm out.

"That's my daughter that's been taken."

"Let him through," Dakota said. She was standing in the doorway. Janice's home was a two-story clapboard house with a black roof and a double garage. The moment he entered he was immediately met by the chief and several neighbors who knew Janice. Janice had a cut on her forehead. The blood was dry. She was nursing a bruised face with an ice pack when he caught sight of her.

"Ben," Janice got up but then nearly toppled over. An officer tried to keep her upright. "I'm so sorry, I tried to protect her."

"What happened?"

Janice was about to explain but Dakota offered to fill in the blanks. "An intruder entered through a side window. We're not sure if he was planning to rape her or take her but Janice—"

"I heard this moan, it was so small like a child. I thought it was the dog at first. It was after one in the morning. I got up and went to check on Chloe, you know just in case she was having another one of her bad dreams. That's when I saw him." Her face was full of fear as she tried to recall what happened. "He was leaning over her, he had this huge knife. I turned the light on and that's when he came at me."

"You're certain it was a man?"

"He was wearing a mask but I heard his voice. I asked him what the hell he was doing."

"What did he say?"

She hesitated to reply. "Collecting." She stared at Ben as though she was looking right through him. It often happened with victims as they recalled a traumatic event. They relived it in their mind. Her hand was shaking, her lip quivered as a single tear streaked her cheek.

"Ben," Dakota gestured for them to speak outside. He was still looking at his mother-in-law in disbelief. He couldn't blame her. How does a sixty-two-year-old woman fight off a man with a blade? God, he had been so foolish to let her out of his sight. He knew it was a bad idea letting her stay over. She'd been doing it for the past three months. Weekends. She wanted to get out as much as Janice wanted to see her. The therapist had said it would be good for her. That it was time to give her room to breathe. He couldn't prevent her from going places, she'd said.

"I want to see the room," Ben said, moving up the stairs while Dakota followed. As he entered the bedroom he looked at the unmade bed. The duvet was lying on the ground. Spots of blood were on the floor.

"His?"

"We're going to check."

A chill came over him. Rage consumed his mind as he thought about someone snatching his daughter. Whoever it was had taken one hell of a risk. Did they know she was his? Ben's eyes scanned the floor, walls, and window. He moved to the window and looked out across the yard towards the tree line.

"She was knocked unconscious. It could have been worse, Ben," Dakota said.

"Worse? What's worse than having my daughter taken?"

He heard what she said but at the same time his mind was rolling through what happened. That's what he did. He placed himself in the shoes of the kidnapper and reversed the event in his mind.

"Show me where he got in."

Dakota didn't even hesitate, she turned and took him back downstairs to the mud room where the window was. There was damage around the lock. He'd pried it open.

"What about prints?" He turned to her. "Where is the crime scene investigation unit?"

"You're looking at it. Along with a few other officers."

"What?"

“This kind of thing rarely happens here. Heck, most people feel comfortable leaving their doors and windows unlocked.”

His anger was getting the better of him. It was clouding his judgment and derailing his line of thinking. He was used to having everything at his disposal. Of course small towns didn’t have the resources, usually these things were handled by state police, or they would call in the CSI unit from a neighboring town that was larger.

“I need everyone out of here now and we need to check for fibers.”

“What the hell is going on here?” Chief Danvers walked in while Ben was examining the window.

“Oh, Ben, this is Kurt Danvers, our chief. Chief, Benjamin Forrester. FBI.”

“FBI?”

The chief’s eyes widened then narrowed.

“Well, that’s not exactly true,” Ben muttered, not even turning to acknowledge him. “I’m on leave, or maybe I’m retired. I haven’t decided yet.”

Ben turned and looked over his well-polished appearance.

"Sir, look, I'm sorry what's happened to your daughter, and you have our word we'll investigate this thoroughly, but this is now an official crime scene and…"

"You don't want me to fuck it up? Kind of late now that you've had your officers traipsing through here."

"Mr. Forrester," Danvers said.

"Ben."

"Where were you last night?"

Ben continued studying the window, showing little attention to the chief.

"At home."

"Can anyone verify that?"

He turned slowly. "Are you suggesting that I was involved in this?"

"It's a question."

"Well, here's your answer."

Ben flipped him the bird. Dakota smirked; the chief however didn't find it amusing.

"I'm going to need you and your mother-in-law to come down to the station."

Ben scoffed. "Are you kidding me?"

"Until we can determine what has happened here—"

"You need to focus on those who are closest, because, of course statistics tell you that only a tiny minority of kidnapped children are taken by strangers." Ben knew what he was going to say. It was like a bad record.

Chief Danvers's eyes darted between Dakota and him.

Ben sniffed. "Perhaps that's why you haven't caught this man already. And, if you actually had paid attention to the photos of the victims, maybe this wouldn't have happened."

"Crime photos?" the chief looked at Ben with a frown on his face.

"Yes, the ones I was looking at last night, when you assume I was here kidnapping my own daughter."

Chief Danvers cleared his throat. "Woods, a moment." He walked out. Dakota grimaced; Ben figured she hadn't told him. A short distance from the room he could hear

Danvers grilling her.

"You know I could take your badge for that? What on earth are you doing giving our private police reports to him?"

"I think he can help, chief."

"You don't get to make that decision. Now I would advise you to tread carefully."

Dakota came back into the room.

Ben breathed in deeply at the thought of this predator watching his daughter. What was he doing with her now? Where was she? All his nightmares came back and bore down on him with a crushing blow. It didn't matter that the M.O. didn't fit Henri Bruns — that was the first person he assumed responsible when Janice told him she was gone. Racing over here all he could think about was him returning to finish what he had started.

"Any other neighbors report seeing or hearing anything suspicious?" Ben asked.

"We have officers out canvassing the homes now, and we've blocked off Route 3. But no word so far."

Everything inside him wanted to tell everyone to get out. The thought that someone might screw up the crime scene, taint evidence, or move an item was beyond troubling.

"We need to get started."

He was used to entering chaos and having to sort through the dross but this was coming at him too fast. He fished into his pocket and pulled out headache medication. His one hand trembled as he twisted off the lid and pills dropped to the floor. He yelled and tossed the empty plastic container across the room. Dakota stood silent for a second and then began picking the pills up.

"Leave them. Just leave them."

"Ben, listen, the chief—"

He cut her off before she could finish. "You wanted my help. You've got it. I'll handle Danvers," he said before leaving her standing and walking back to where Janice was. One of the other officers had brought her a hot cup of tea. She was still crying. He knew she was blaming herself, and what it felt like to bear guilt and mull over the things you should have done differently. He'd been doing it for over two years.

He crouched and palmed her hands in his own. "Janice. I'm gonna find the man who did this. We'll get Chloe back."

Chapter 17

Down the dark cavernous tunnel he carried her limp body over his right shoulder. Gravel crunched beneath his boots as he trudged deeper into the depths of what was a paradise to him. Unconscious she didn't feel his hand slide up beneath her shorts and over the curve of her cheek. She was like an early Christmas gift to himself, one that couldn't be opened for a few days. It was all part of the excitement. Logic told him to rush, check her skin, have his way and then if she wasn't right, dump her body but where was the fun in that?

He was sure she could stay.

It wasn't like the police were going to find him. He had this fine-tuned. His mind drifted back to the girl's room. Even though that bitch interfered she was no match for him. How quickly she dropped. He chuckled at the thought. He'd considered lingering inside the house — taking his time, pushing the risk level as far as he could. This was exactly what he needed. Taking them from the forest had become too easy, the excitement had waned. But this, oh this was a new level of exhilaration. Sure, he'd broken his method of operation but that's what would confuse them. As he reached a large metal door with a bolt, he unlatched it and swung it open. It groaned for oil.

He wasn't sure how long he would keep her. That depended on her. How compliant and responsive she was to his every command. As he laid her down on the bed, he took a step back and reveled in his handiwork. Why had he waited this long to take people from their homes? It was even easier than campsites. Numerous times he had run into park rangers or hikers who were in the wrong place at the wrong time. Thankfully he knew the terrain better than any of them.

What would it be like to be caught? He'd mulled it over in his mind, closing his eyes. No, not yet. There were more women to be snatched, tortured, and brought to the very brink of death. More to add to his collection. He had considered taking the other woman. He laughed, remembering the look on her face. Who the hell are you? She was pathetically slow. One swift blow to the head and she was out cold.

He stepped closer to gaze at the girl. She was so quiet and still. He placed his hands around her small throat and felt a sexual rush as he began to squeeze lightly. He released. Not now. Wait. Hold off. It's so much better when they are awake and looking at you. You become God to them; he told himself. You are the giver and taker of life. He turned and walked to the corner of the room where he kept additional zip ties. He snapped them between his hands, making sure they would hold before proceeding to wrap one around an ankle and then the iron bedpost. Once he was done, he couldn't resist running his fingers up her legs over her top and squeezing her perfect mounds. She was definitely special; a perfect addition to his collection.

He got down on his knees and inhaled her scent, getting high off the natural aroma of her light body mist.

He pulled out his blade and sliced away at her silky bedroom shorts until she was fully exposed. Continuing up with the blade he tore through the thin white T-shirt until her white bra was showing. One quick snap and her breasts billowed out. Seventeen and as ripe as can be. He gazed at her nakedness, his pulse racing and arousal taking over.

He licked his lips and willed himself to stay calm and not touch her. But he had to at least see if she could stay longer than twenty-four hours. He paced back and forth for a second, grunted, and then flipped her on her side. His eyes scanned back and forth.

Perfect. Her skin was absolutely perfect. Turning her over, he could barely hold in his excitement as he finished restraining her. The very thought of how it would look got him hard.

Pulling back from the bed, he took a seat on a chair in the corner of the room to gaze at her flesh. It was exquisite. No tattoos. No birthmarks, or skin modifications. He pictured in his mind what she would look like alongside the others. Maybe this time she would be the one.

Only time would tell.

Chapter 18

Chief Danvers was trying to get the media under control. It wasn't working. Keeping a kidnapping under wrap wasn't easy with social media. Locals tweeting about police on scene had got others curious. Neighbors had shown up outside Janice Turner's house. Then, of course, there was all the attention from the Taylor girl who had been found dead and her friend Helen Hayes who was still missing. This was spiraling out of control fast. He stood behind a podium in front of the department trying to hush the group of reporters standing a few feet from him. A few officers, including Dakota Woods, stood beside him. Local news, crews from Ellsworth, and even as far as Boston were gathered to hear good news. He didn't have it. Most were holding out their phones, snapping shots and looking to be the first to snag the story.

"On Friday at approximately eight a.m., park rangers

came across the body of a female at the foot of Mount Champlain in Acadia National Park. It is currently being treated as suspicious. We have not released the identity and nor will we be discussing the details at this time. Our team of highly qualified officers are currently following up on leads at which point we'll be able to provide more information."

"Is the missing Hayes girl linked to the latest kidnapping?"

Danvers looked at Dakota then back at the reporter who'd asked. "Whoever is responsible for this will be apprehended and be brought to justice here in Maine. That's all I can tell you right now."

The reporters grumbled and protested as Danvers stepped away from the mics clustered together.

"Chief, I need a word," Dakota tried to get his attention.

He continued moving towards the door at a fair clip as cameras flashed. "Not now."

* * *

Ben had spent the better part of the day down at the station answering questions. As they didn't have any reason to hold him, they let him loose. After getting out of the station, he drove Janice to the home of a friend in Tremont who had offered to have her stay there for a while. The line of questioning at the station was to be expected. They had been through his house and removed computers. While this monster had his child they were wasting time searching for dirt on him.

Ben returned to Janice's home with his mind full of questions. It was dark now and as he drove down the long road that was hedged by dense trees he could see porch lights glimmering. Where was he that night? Why her? Was it random? No, he'd forced his way into the house. He was determined to have her. *You were looking at her, weren't you, before that night?* he thought to himself.

He parked in the driveway and let himself in. He felt around for the light switch and turned it on. He'd been to Janice's house many times at night but even he found himself bumping into furniture. She loved antique items, the more the better. Wherever there was space, she found something to stick in there. *You must have had a flashlight.* Ben went into the kitchen and searched the counters and drawers for a flashlight. Not finding one he went into the garage and found one in the toolbox.

He hit the button and gave it a few smacks with the side of his hand to get it to shine. After turning on all the lights in the house, he ventured out back using the side door on the garage. He wanted to see what the intruder had. He sniffed the air. Ben gave the sliding doors a tug. Locked. Had any of the neighbors seen a light through the trees the way he'd seen their porch lights? Even if they had, he doubted it would have given them cause for concern.

Ben walked backwards from the house, casting a glance at each of the windows. A police cruiser drove by. He'd told them that he would be staying at Janice's house for the night and that more than likely they would see him puttering around with a flashlight. The last thing he wanted was some rookie cop shooting him in the middle of the night.

The two-story house was perched up on a mound of earth. At the furthest part of the yard you couldn't see directly into the windows above. He would have wanted to have a clear view of the comings and goings. A six-foot cedar fence wrapped around the property line to prevent the dog from getting out.

The dog, Jasper. It was alive when he arrived but docile. He'd forgot to ask Janice about that. Had he drugged the dog? There was no way that dog would have let anyone in without barking up a storm. It wasn't trained like Jinx but it wasn't friendly to strangers. In fact, that was the only reason why he was willing to let his daughter stay at her home. It gave him a sense of peace knowing Jasper was there but now he realized it had been pointless.

He walked to the back gate and unlocked it. It took him directly back into Acadia's woods. It was dark and dense. A perfect place to stay hidden out of sight and observe. He turned and shook his head. No, the fence was in the way. He surveyed the area for a tree that might be easy to climb — something with low-hanging branches. Finding two, he tucked the flashlight in his back pocket and climbed. It had been years since he had done that. Making it up he could see the house but it wasn't a perfect view. Back on the ground he tried the next. He tried another. Still no good, but it did reveal something in the tree beside him. He made his way down and then climbed the second tree. Sure enough, broken limbs — now that gave him a wide shot of the house. A chill came over him thinking that hours earlier, he'd been sitting here.

Ben remained there for ten minutes staring at the house. Mosquitoes buzzed around his head like mini RC helicopters. Fireflies flashed inside bushes in front of the house. Why this one? Did he come out here on weekends? That would have been the only time Chloe was present and she'd only been here over the past three months. But the police reports said the previous women who'd been taken were hikers and campers. Chloe did neither. She hated mosquitoes. The other women were taken from campgrounds and in the middle of Acadia. Why did you come to the border of the forest unless you were looking to increase the risk factor? *You're bored, aren't you?* he thought to himself. The thrill was in the risk of being caught. Ben chewed it over in his mind. There may have only been seven known to the police, but he was convinced there were more. He'd taken more women and grown tired of what he was finding in the woods. This allowed him to observe, to see them undress, and to look at their skin.

Ben raked the light over the bark on the tree where he might have torn a piece away. With all that pent-up frustration and sexual energy it wasn't uncommon to come across traces of semen left behind.

Back at the house he looked at the area where he'd entered. Police had tried for prints but didn't find any. None on the doorknobs, the side walls, or the pane itself. He'd been wearing gloves. Inside the home Ben went around and switched off the lights until he was cloaked in darkness. He returned to the entry point and moved through the house, noting every creak that the floorboards made. He listened to every nuance that a house this old would make. The thump of the metal ventilator as the air conditioning kicked in. The noise from random cars that might have driven by. Had they seen his flashlight? Was he even using one that night or had he been watching them for so long that he was confident of getting upstairs without bumping into anything? It was possible. As his eyes adjusted to darkness, the edges of objects became visible.

Still, this was new to him. He was used to approaching them on the forest trails. Perhaps crouching down in a bush as a runner, hiker, or bicyclist made their way along the path. Or did he even need to do that? What if he didn't need to hide? It would explain why no one heard anyone scream. How could you blend in with your environment, appear safe and not appear as a threat?

Ben was about to ascend the steps when his phone rang. It startled him and a cold fear flushed through his body.

Chapter 19

There were very few times he'd heard them scream. It was usually in the first few days after he'd brought them back and before he broke them down — that's what it was all about, breaking them down. He wasn't in a rush. You didn't rush these things. He knew about the Stockholm syndrome and used it to his advantage. It was all about getting them to be emotionally attached to him. At least the ones he wanted alive. The others… he snorted, sitting naked at his table creating a new mask to replace the one that had been ruined. This one was much better. It had more wrinkles to it. There was something strangely horrifying about aging. The way skin would lose its suppleness and appear almost as if it was melting off the skull itself.

A police scanner played quietly in the background. Domestics, disputes, all the usual crap that happened in a small town. It kept him one step ahead of them. Police were stupid; they wouldn't follow him into the forest. That kind of recklessness would get them killed.

He'd had a close encounter with one young officer three years ago. Now that was one he would have liked in his collection. She had guts. Pity that bear trap took her leg out otherwise she might have been someone he would have enjoyed playing games with. He'd considered going back and releasing the trap and taking her but common sense prevailed.

Taking the new mask, he slipped it over his face and admired it. It fit like a glove and smelled fresh. Completely naked he danced slowly, hearing music playing in his mind.

All around him hanging on the walls were animal heads, every single one of them he'd hunted and killed himself. Deer, raccoons, wolves, bear, all the way down to small animals like rabbits and squirrels.

That's how it had started.

Hunting humans — could it be done?

Yes, yes it could.

He reached for a robe behind the door, a black one with a red stripe around the edge. He slipped it on, letting its silky material awaken his senses. Standing barefoot in front of the mirror he admired himself before going out into the tunnel and walking down to the rooms that housed his collection. There were ten, each one naturally formed by the ocean, deep below the Acadia National Forest.

"Now who's going to be the lucky one tonight?" he said, tapping the room doors with excitement while tiptoeing in unison to the music playing inside his head. Swaying, turning, and running his fingers across the metal doors while strumming them, he heard their cries. They knew what was in store. Of course he kept them sedated but not enough that they couldn't know what was going on or feel the fear. Did they fear him? Did they hope he didn't choose them?

He stopped in front of a door and pulled the metal latch back. Inside was a beautiful brunette that he'd taken from a nearby campsite. She'd been here for over a year.

So many times he had considered disposing of her but he just couldn't bring himself to do it. She was too lovely.

Unlocking the door, he cracked it open and leered inside. The look on her face never changed. It was one of terror. She shuffled back as he came in and sealed it shut.

Her screams could be heard filling up the hallway as he slowly approached her.

"Don't worry, you're safe now."

Chapter 20

It was Nate Mueller. Ben jabbed accept and placed the phone to his ear as he continued ascending the stairway. Every few steps it would creak hard.

"Ben. I'm sorry. I just heard. I'm en route as we speak."

His mind was still on the crime. The steps creaked. *How did you pass over these unless you had been in here before or maybe Janice didn't hear you?* To anyone else it might not have mattered but to him it was a part of knowing who he was dealing with. Ben sighed into the phone.

"You think I can get reinstated?" he asked Nate.

"Reinstated, no, it's been too long, but having you work with us, that I can do. Already had the conversation with the powers that be. That is, if you're up to it?"

"Of course I am."

"I should be there within the next couple of hours. My

flight gets in just after ten."

He continued moving through the hallways down to the room where Chloe would have been. Janice's room was next to hers. Suddenly he got a shot of pain in his head. Another migraine was coming on hard. It had been building. It felt like someone was stabbing him.

"I'm going to have to call you back."

Ben hung up, fished into his pocket for his meds and went down to get himself a glass of water. He noticed his hands were shaking. He flipped the lightswitch on.

A question lingered in his mind. *How long did you stay after you had subdued Janice?*

As he stood there mulling it over he heard the front door open. Twisting around, he saw Dakota in the doorway.

"You sure it's a good idea to stay here tonight?" she asked.

"I don't think it matters. I won't be doing much sleeping tonight." He sighed. "Anyway, I'm not staying."

It was hard to function knowing Chloe was out there

with a madman. The thought of what he'd done to her or was doing was liable to send him over the edge. He couldn't go there in his mind. He had to stay focused, clearheaded.

"Any leads?" he asked.

She shook her head. "No."

It wasn't the news he wanted. But then someone like this wasn't going to make mistakes.

"How do you think he took her out of here?" she asked.

"Through the woods. With all the police on the roads since the Hayes girl, he wouldn't have risked it."

"You think he drugged her?"

Ben nodded.

"What direction do we go with this?" she asked.

"We need to find the connection; something that ties them all together. I need a record of everyone who has gone missing in the park over the past five years, and can you speak with the coroner? I want to see the body."

She pulled out a phone. "Yeah, I'll make a few calls."

He'd had his eyes closed for a while just allowing the medication to take hold. The memories of that day in the Everglades played over in his mind. He couldn't lose her.

"Right, thanks, I'll see you in ten." He heard Dakota wrap up the call.

"Managed to get the coroner to come in on his day off. Let me give you fair warning, he's not exactly the kind of person you might imagine. Oh, and don't ask him about the scar."

Ben ran a hand over his face. "Let's go."

* * *

They took Dakota's car. On the way over he could tell Dakota was itching for answers on the Henri Bruns case.

"Go on. Ask away."

"About what?"

"The Bruns case. Ever since we've met you've been eager to ask me but haven't." He pulled up one of his books that was lying on the floor that went into detail on the case.

"He changed his M.O. too, didn't he?" she asked.

"Yeah, but for him it was personal."

"How?"

"We located two of his victims before they died."

"You mean he didn't cut them up?"

Ben looked out the window at the town of Eden Falls as they hung a left into Hancock Street. The glow of lights made everything seem so peaceful but it was far from that. The media had kicked up quite a hornet's nest. Townsfolk were fuming that they had been left in the dark.

"No, not all his victims. He looked for very specific ones. He didn't have the luxury of following them for weeks on end. So the ones that didn't match his specific look were buried alive."

"And you don't think this is personal? I mean Chloe is the first one that's been taken from a home. He went to a lot of trouble to get her."

"He's bored. This risk of getting caught is beginning to excite him."

"Do..."

"Do I think he will kill her?"

Ben looked at her. She gripped the wheel tighter.

"If we don't get to her. Yes."

When they pulled up in front of the medical examiner's office he was waiting for them in his car. Dakota killed the engine. The man who got out was wiry and in a desperate need of a shave. He wore a brown tweed suit and white shirt but without a tie.

"Thanks for coming out, Lennie. This is Benjamin Forrester."

Ben nodded.

"Lennie Sunns."

He greeted them with a handshake, that's when Ben saw the scar down the left side of his face and neck. A knife wound for sure. Lennie led the way in. Inside, he turned on the lights and changed out of his jacket into white scrubs and blue latex gloves. They entered a morgue full of shiny steel doors. Lennie opened one and pulled out the tray, he immediately pulled back the cover to reveal the cleaned-up cadaver of Rachael Taylor.

Lennie stood to one side while Ben and Dakota remained on the other.

"There was no sign of semen. Ligature marks on ankles and wrists were consistent with plastic zip ties. She was strangled using a piece of wire a quarter of an inch thick. She didn't die fast, it was long and drawn out. Signs of vaginal and anal intercourse. She had a fractured skull, but it was strangulation that killed her. The knife wounds seemed to be unnecessary, almost like a form of torture rather than an attempt to kill her. She hadn't eaten anything in a day. Toxicology showed signs of having secobarbital sodium in the system. She also had traces of formaldehyde and glycerin."

Dakota jotted notes down on a pad of paper. Ben walked around the tray and looked at the bottom of her feet, around her ankles and legs. There were scrapes and cuts.

"How old do you think these are?" Ben asked.

"A few days," he replied.

"Anything under the nails?"

"Nothing."

"How much of the formaldehyde and glycerin did you find?" Dakota asked.

"I won't have an exact figure on that for a day or two."

Ben nodded, taking it all in. He looked a little closer at the side of her face. Using a pen, he pushed back some hair.

"What you got?"

Just behind her ear was a tattoo of three small black birds.

"In the report, the other women had marks on the body, didn't they?"

"Yeah. Birthmarks, body modification, and tattoos."

* * *

As they left the building heading back to the vehicle, Dakota stopped.

"Do you think there's a connection with the marks?"

"Possibly. Look into formaldehyde and glycerin. See what you can dig up on that."

Dakota gave him a lift back to Janice's place to pick up

his truck.

"The headaches, how long have you had them?" she asked.

"Two years."

"You still have nightmares?"

Ben cast her a sideways glance.

"My father was a cop in Boston, he saw a lot of bad shit. I used to hear him at night."

"How did he cope?" Ben asked.

She turned to him. "He shot himself. With his police-issued handgun." The car pulled into the driveway, she breathed out hard while it idled.

"Well on that note…" Ben pushed out of the car. He was in the process of closing the door when she spoke again.

"Ben."

"Yeah?" he leaned in through the window.

"I'm sorry."

He nodded slowly, offered back a strained expression and went inside.

Chapter 21

Making his way back to his home off Route 3, Ben Forrester was thinking about how he was going to catch this guy with so little evidence to go on. It wasn't like the women were hookers. The girls weren't local so they had to leave the investigating to police in their hometown until the FBI showed up. All they had right now was a dead body and a handful of reports from previous abductions.

Chloe. The memory of her last words burned him.

"Love you, Dad, see you Sunday night."

He was thinking about the dead body when he turned the corner into his property. A black SUV was parked at an angle. Sitting on the step was Nate Mueller. He glanced up, blew out some cigarette smoke, and waited for Ben to pull in.

They had known each other since the academy. While others didn't want to advance up the chain of command because it just meant more shit they had to deal with, Nate did. He'd always had his eyes set on promotion. Eventually he became Ben's supervisor. That was an odd time but it worked.

"Ben," he waited until he was out of the vehicle before he showed him the eighteen-year-old whiskey. It was how they kicked off every case and part of the reason Ben had ended up drinking too much.

He met him on the steps with a part handshake, part hug. Nate handed him the bottle. He glanced at it. It was Macallan 1997 18-Year-Old Sherry Oak. At one hundred and twenty-seven dollars a bottle, most might have waited for a celebration — that wasn't how it worked with them. It had become almost like a rabbit's foot. They had caught every single perp after drinking that stuff. On the Henri Bruns case the bottle was dropped accidentally. Call it what you will but to them it was not a good sign as it turned out they never caught him.

"Come on in."

No one could have prepared him for the loss. Ben got

into the FBI to catch them, not to wind up as bait but in many ways that's what special agents were. Bait for the sick and depraved.

He tossed his keys on the counter and pulled down two glasses from the drink cabinet.

"Quite the place you've got here," Nate said.

"It's not much. But it's home."

"Just wish I could have visited under better circumstances. How are you holding up?"

Ben never replied. He didn't need to. He took the whiskey and carefully twisted off the cap and poured out two fingers. That was the answer.

Truth be told, how he handled any kidnapping was different each time depending on who had been taken. Kids were the worst. Some might have thought that he should be sobbing on the floor or out there running in the woods searching for Chloe. But that wasn't reality. He was no good to her in a mess. He had to think straight, fight the urge to break down.

Dad, I can handle it, her words drummed in his mind.

He had to believe she could. For all he knew she might have escaped like the Taylor girl. At least that was the hope he clung to.

Nate got straight down to business. That was his strong point. He didn't mince words. In the bureau, tracking kidnappings, murders, and serial killings was the norm. It wasn't that you became numb to it but it was a part of an investigator's daily workload.

"What have we got so far?"

Ben brought him up to speed on what they had. He handed him the reports.

"You look tired," Ben said. "You should get some sleep."

"I'll sleep when I'm dead."

That was always his answer, and it was true. The guy was a machine. Both of them at one point were tossing back smart pills just to function. Modafinil twice a day and they were good for twenty-four hours. Nate had got him on them. Up until then energy came in a cup, or a can.

Ben sat in silence, sipping on his drink and watching Nate flip through the file. He thought over some of the cases they'd been on and the ones who were the hardest to catch. Tracking serial killers wasn't easy, at least those who didn't plan on getting caught. They didn't operate like most killers. The smart ones avoided detection in ten different ways. They never left DNA at the scene; they had no relationship with their victim; they chose their victims from areas where they didn't live; they used guns that weren't registered; they made sure not to take any trophies, touch the body, or leave behind a mess, and they usually struck in the early hours of the morning when people were asleep. Everything was taken into consideration; wearing gloves, buying vehicles ahead of time, paying in cash, destroying receipts, and setting everything that could be traced back to them on fire. If they were careful, they didn't need an alibi as no one would even suspect them.

But even the smart ones slipped up, you just had to hope you were there when they did.

Once Nate was done, he tossed the folder to one side.

"Seems our guy is going to a lot of trouble to take someone from the town, you think this person is related to Bruns?"

"No," Ben shook his head. "But I think he lives and works on the island. He knows these woods."

"Have the police interviewed rangers, camp staff, someone who might have been able to blend in?"

"They haven't done much of anything, Nate. I get the feeling they were hoping this was all just going to go away. They aren't prepared for this."

"Well they had better get it together."

"Did the bureau just send you?"

"There should be a few from the Bangor department down here tomorrow for the briefing. By the way, I should give you this."

Nate got up and went over to his luggage. He unzipped a side pocket and came back holding in his hand a holster with a Glock 22. He flashed gold; it was Ben's old badge. When he had taken leave he handed it all in with every intention of not returning. Had he been any other FBI agent they wouldn't be doing this, but his track record and expertise in catching criminals was enough reason for them to agree with Nate.

"You still know how to shoot one," Nate said half-jokingly.

"I guess we'll find out."

It was virtually impossible to forget how to shoot. It was like riding a bike. Besides, it was drummed into them at the academy. They put them through hours of target practice, pulling it from the holster, and dealing with misfires and jams. By the time they left that thing was a part of them. An extension of who they were.

"You want another drink?"

"Sure," Nate replied.

Ben began pouring when his phone buzzed. He immediately grabbed it, hoping it was Chloe. It was Dakota.

"You ready for this?" she asked.

"What you got?"

"The formaldehyde and glycerin together are often used in preventing tissue shrinkage. Essentially it's a method of preserving and protecting used by taxidermists."

"Where can you buy that?" he asked.

"Online. Your local pharmacy does both. But it doesn't make any sense. Why would she have that inside of her?"

"Depends what our guy is doing with them or does for a living."

"You don't think…"

"Believe me, Woods. I've come across worse."

"What time's the briefing?" he asked.

"Nine."

"Right, see you then," Dakota said before hanging up. Ben stood there holding the phone in his hand for a moment. His mind churning over. It shifted back and forth from the present to the past.

"Who was that?" Nate asked.

"Officer Dakota Woods. Lead investigator on the

case."

"Good-looking woman?"

Ben snorted. Nate wasn't married. The closest he'd got to it was getting engaged to a girl from California. But she wanted him to quit the bureau. He wasn't going to do that. It was what kept him alive. Ben couldn't see Nate doing anything else. He was made for it.

That evening Nate stayed at his place. He put him in the guest room. After he'd turned in, Ben went into Chloe's room. He glanced around at her belongings. The room smelled of her. In his mind he could hear her voice, her laughter, and the sound of her guitar. He walked over to it and ran his fingers over the strings. It was usually kept in a black case but that Saturday she'd left it in the corner. He let out a heavy sigh and headed into his room. After splashing water over his face, and rubbing his tired eyes, he lay back on the bed and tried to catch a few hours.

He must have dozed off for an hour or two when he was awoken by the sound of his phone buzzing and jiggling around on the side table. He reached over and hit accept without even looking to see who it was.

He cleared his throat. "Yeah?"

There was heavy breathing on the other end of the line.

Ben asked again, "Woods?"

"Hello, Dr. Forrester," the male voice said.

"Who is this?"

The person snorted on the other end. "Oh I feel hurt, after all we've been through together."

A trickle of fear crept over him.

"You know, I've thought about you a lot since that day, have you thought about me?"

Ben glanced at his phone, hoping to see a number but there was none. "What do you want?"

"You know how hard it was to find you? But then when I heard about the lovely Chloe."

Ben bolted upright in bed, his eyes widening

"Bruns?"

"Tell me, Ben, did you think it was me who took her?"

Ben had no words.

"Come now, you were never at a loss for words when you were pursuing me. What's happened? Don't tell me you've lost your edge. I must say it's been rather boring without you around. These other agents just don't have that touch." He breathed in deeply. "They're amateurs. Not like us, Ben."

"How did you get this number?"

"Please. Give me some credit."

"Where are you?"

He let out a small chuckle. "Close, but don't worry, Ben, I'm not going to pay you a visit anytime soon."

"Why not? I would love the company."

He let out a laugh.

"Listen, I feel awful about Elizabeth and Adam."

"Am I meant to believe that?"

"Ben. Just because I have a taste for blood, it doesn't mean I don't feel loss like you. What has it been like? Do you have trouble sleeping at night? Do you see her in your dreams?"

"No. I see you with a bullet in your head."

"Ah now that's the Ben I knew."

"Why are you calling?"

"Curiosity. Boredom, maybe I just like hearing the sound of your voice."

"Night, asshole."

"Hold on, Ben, let's not be hasty. I'm sure you want to see Chloe again?"

"What do you mean?"

"Oh I think you know."

Ben grit his teeth. "I'm done with you."

"Did you know, Ben, that I could have taken Chloe that night but I didn't? I spared her. Do you know why?"

Ben remained silent. His mind in turmoil.

"Because I knew if I took her, it would destroy you and I can't have that. No, you still have answers for me. You and I are a team, we're alike."

"I'm nothing like you."

He chuckled on the other end of the phone.

"To catch me, you had to think like me."

"But I didn't catch you."

"Not in the sense that I'm locked away. But you did find out who I was."

"Is Henri Bruns even your name?"

"You tell me, Ben."

Ben noticed his hand was shaking. He pulled at the bedside drawer and removed a mickey bottle full of whiskey. He glanced at his badge and gun beside him.

"Enough with your games," Ben said.

"But we're only getting started."

The line went dead.

Chapter 22

"The nerve of the animal," Nate said as they walked into the Eden Falls Police Station the next morning. Both of them were holding coffees. "He's toying with you."

"No, he thinks he will learn how I stumbled onto his crimes through his dialogue with me."

"You're not going to listen to him, are you? I say we put a trace on your phone."

"Nate, right now my daughter is out there, perhaps dead for all I know. All I care about is finding this sicko and ending this."

The room was full of police as well as the medical examiner and the mayor of Eden Falls. Chief Danvers and Dakota were at the front along with two people from the Maine Warden Service who had come in to offer assistance and insights into previous search-and-rescues.

Bangor FBI had already obtained the photos of the victims. They were attached to a wall at the front of the room. Several photos were enlarged to highlight wounds on the Taylor girl's body. The chief provided a rundown of what the coroner had put in his report then turned it over to Nate. Nate went up front and tried to get the attention of a dozen officers who were joking around.

"Do you find this funny?" he said to one of them who was making light of the death. He went a shade of red before Nate continued. He invited Ben up.

"This is Dr. Benjamin Forrester, he will be working on this case. If he needs anything you are to get it, do I make myself clear?"

There was no animosity between the police and the bureau as some might imagine, in many ways the FBI agents were making their life easy by showing up and working the case.

"Do you have anything to add?" Nate asked Ben.

He nodded. "We need to start with the park rangers and camp employees, there is a good chance our perp is someone who works in the National Park Service."

"How do you figure that?" one officer asked.

"Are there witness reports of anyone forcing our victims out of the forest? Did anyone hear screams? No. Seven vanished, but they aren't the only ones. We have reports going back another four years. There is a strong possibility that he was just warming up. One a year for four years then that changed to two. If we don't catch him that will increase to three or more next year."

"Those other women weren't found," a man from the Maine Warden Service said. The Maine Warden Service was the law enforcement agency that was usually pulled in when any search-and-rescue operations occurred. They had specialty teams that dealt in aviation, special investigation, and forensic mapping.

"And you are?"

"Ted Bishop."

"Well, Ted, that doesn't mean they aren't alive. It just means our perp has a very specific taste." Ben turned and tapped each of the photos of the women that had been found.

"Every single one of them had a mark on them.

Tattoo, birthmark, or body implant. All of them were found with traces of formaldehyde and glycerin in their system as well as secobarbital sodium which means he is drugging them and possibly has some ties to taxidermy. I want you to get out there and find out who might be involved in that, check the pharmacies to see if anyone has bought a large amount of formaldehyde and glycerin."

Ben went on to provide a profile of the suspect while Dakota and Nate handed out sheets to officers. "It's our belief that we are dealing with someone who is from the area, hasn't had any run-ins with the law, and may even be known by some of you in this room."

Chief Danvers came up front. He didn't seem impressed by the fact that the FBI were involved.

"I'm not sure if anyone has told you this yet but we have already done interviews with neighbors in the area."

"And?" Ben shot back.

"A few of them mentioned that someone had attempted to break the locks on their windows. Now we are pretty certain this is the same individual. The team will be checking for prints today."

"So you think it was random?" Nate asked.

"That's my thoughts," Danvers replied.

"What about the dog?" someone asked.

"He was drugged."

"Why not just kill it?"

Ben paused before replying, it was long enough for one of the officers to continue.

"Maybe he's an animal lover."

"No. He's just careful," Ben added.

An officer replied, "Breaking into a house doesn't seem too careful to me."

"Have you found him yet? Found any prints? Don't underestimate this man."

The fact was they had very little on him. A footprint had been found near the area of Janice's house but it had no tread to it. They could work out the size of the shoe to be around size thirteen but that didn't mean anything. Ben believed that he was wearing something custom. Something that couldn't be traced to any shoes he owned.

It was very possible that he had stuffed the inside of the shoe to make it appear that he was a size thirteen when he may have been smaller. He had given a lot of thought to what could or couldn't be tracked back to him.

As they were about to leave Chief Danvers asked if he could have a word. Nate said he would meet up later for lunch. Ben and Dakota entered Danvers's office. It was a cramped space with a small wooden table that had a picture of his family on it. Every single thing in that office was in order. Papers pulled together, a filing system for folders, a pen holder, and a small office-sized putting green.

"Do you play golf, Ben?" Danvers asked.

"Not really."

He raised his eyebrows before taking a shot using a miniature club.

"It lets me think. I can't be out on the green, so this is the next best thing."

Dakota looked at Ben and rolled her eyes.

"Listen, I don't think we got off on the right foot. I'm

sorry about what happened to your daughter and we will do our best to find her."

"How long have you been chief?" Ben asked.

"Ten years. This is a first for us."

"Even after all those disappearances?" Ben asked.

"Disappearances happen, Ben. We do our best to find them but some people don't want to be found. We had a man three years ago who parked his vehicle near Acadia and disappeared. He was later found to be living in Las Vegas. Like I said, some people just want to get away and there's no better place to fake your death than in a national park. Others? Well, it's treacherous terrain out there. I mean compared to other national parks I think ours fares pretty well."

There was a knock at the door.

"Excuse me, chief, looks like we have a second body."

Ben spun around in his chair, his pulse began to race.

Chapter 23

Fear could paralyze you or push you forward. Right now Ben was using it to get out the door. The thought of Chloe's body flashed through his mind. Was it her? *Please don't let it be her.*

Ben, Dakota, and Nate followed the chief and other officers. The ride out to Duck Brook Bridge in the north end of the island was nerve-wracking. No details had been shared about who the woman was. All that could be heard was the sound of sirens blaring. Cars veered to one side to let them through.

Dakota looked at Ben. No one wanted to say it but everyone was thinking it. Could it be Chloe? The only description given was long dark hair. As they got closer Dakota gave everyone a rundown of the place. The bridge had three archways and four turret-style viewing platforms at the top. The bridge itself was part of the Duck Brook carriage road trailhead. The only way you could reach it was on foot. They drove down a road with the same name and turned off to an area that was blocked by a steel gate.

Police and EMS were on site when they arrived. Red and blue lights flashed as they stopped. Bangor FBI were parked slightly up from the trail. They had already cordoned off the area and police were doing their best to hold back several hikers.

The first question that came out of Ben's mouth once out of the car was who found her. An officer pointed to a park ranger. He was a skinny kid dressed in a gray uniform with a shiny gold badge. He was wearing the typical park ranger outfit, which included a Stetson hat, black pants, and boots. He stood off to one side speaking with an officer. He glanced momentarily at Ben as he walked by.

"I want to speak to him before we leave."

It was hard to imagine that these murders were going on right underneath their noses — or that someone had been classing them as accidents but that's what made this so easy for the madman. Ben didn't want to look and yet at the same time he needed to know. Following Dakota to the edge he glanced over. All he could see was a dark mass at the bottom. They had partly covered her with a white sheet. For someone looking on, it just looked as though she'd fallen.

"Around this way," Dakota walked over to the rocky embankment that led down to the brook. The sound of rushing water got louder as they carefully descended the steep slope. Stones broke away and Ben had to brace himself on a tree branch. The chances of a hiker coming down here were slim unless they had a death wish.

All the memories of finding the body buried beneath the earth came flooding back in. A mixture of fear and horror bombarded his senses.

Please don't be her.

All around them were tall pines. At the bottom Ted Bishop was there, along with Danvers and two other officers. Danvers was looking under the sheet when they approached. Nate and Ben waded out into the water and

Danvers pulled it back.

Ben closed his eyes, took a deep breath, and looked.

"Is it her?" Danvers asked.

He breathed a sigh of relief then shook his head. "No."

* * *

An hour later the body was identified. An officer filled them in. "Patricia Welling, a local. Twenty-two, went to Boston University, lived with her single mother on the west side of the island. Was reported missing three years ago."

Ben shook his head then rubbed his eyes. Unless the reports were wrong, that would make her the first local woman. He crouched down beside her and looked at her neck. There were no ligature marks except on her hands and feet. Her body was bloated and skin was absent of color. The odor that came off was pungent and foul.

"Was she strangled?" Dakota asked.

"Doesn't look like it." She was fully dressed in what any hiker would wear. She even had a bag on her back. Ben snapped on a latex glove and pressed her skin and moved her arm. The body still had rigor mortis, which meant she'd died within the past thirty-six hours as that was how long it took for it to leave the body. There was no damage to the skin, no animals had feasted on it which led Ben to believe she couldn't have been here longer than twenty-four hours.

"What can you tell me about this guy who found her?"

"Douglas Adams. Local guy, early twenties, no record of being in trouble with the law except for selling marijuana when he was a kid," Dakota said.

"Get her over to the medical examiner. Find out if our guy has had sex with her and if they can find any hairs, semen, or DNA at all," Nate said.

"Highly doubt it. The last one was clean," Ben said.

"But he's having sex with them."

"Maybe he wears something, shaves, or uses an object to tear them. For all we know he might not even be having sex with them. It's possible they are getting those tears from whatever he is doing to them."

Nate furrowed his brow. "You think he's into

bondage?"

"It's possible. Hooks or some other kind of implement could cause those tears."

Ben rose to his feet and stared down at her. She was beautiful. A woman that could have easily been in a magazine or made a career out of modeling. The question was why did he kill her three years later? She had been one of the women that had gone missing but had never been found until now. Dakota made a few notes on a pad.

"He's keeping them somewhere but where?" Nate asked.

"Has to be local. Possibly in this forest. Are there any homes in the forest itself?"

"Yeah, of course. Cottages and cabins all over the place."

"We need to start checking those. Going door-to-door." An officer stepped in, shaking his head. "That's going to take some time."

"Well, you better get started then," Ben snapped before turning and walking away.

Chapter 24

Light stabbed her eyes.

Chloe Forrester's eyelids fluttered as she began to stir. It was like awakening from a heavy hangover. She wanted to be sick. Her stomach felt as if she had swallowed one too many headache pills. She blinked hard trying to clear the mind fog.

Her wrists and ankles ached, burned even. As the room came into view, it looked as if she was inside a cave. The ceiling above her couldn't have been more than seven feet. It wasn't anything that had been made by human hands. It was rough, jagged, and damp. She could hear the sound of water dripping as she tried to move.

A flood of memories came in. The figure. The masked face approaching her in the darkness. The sheer horror and then a light turning on and Janice's voice.

She glanced at her body. She was covered but not entirely. She was naked beneath the covers and sore. If he had stripped her, what else could he have done? Suddenly, she had this sick feeling that whoever had taken her had raped her. Where was she? She had no recollection of arriving.

Her mouth was dry. She tried to croak out a cry for help but nothing came out. Again she tried, this time it came out and echoed off the walls. There was no reply. "Please, is anyone there?"

This couldn't be happening, not to her. She wanted to call for her dad, but no one could hear her here, wherever here was. Dread crept over her like a slow-moving mist. *I've got to get out of here.* She turned her head to the side and saw that her wrists were bound by plastic zip ties. There was no chance of getting out of these. The more you tugged the tighter they became. Small plastic notches kept them from being undone. The only way you could get these off was to cut them. It might have been different if they had tied her hands together. There were ways to break out of ties that her father had shown her but this was impossible.

Every muscle in her body ached. Her head ached. How long had she been here? What day was it? She remembered small snippets of information as if awakening from a dream only to find herself thrust back in. An old man leaning over her, a hood, trees, and… it was just a blur, blending together.

The room she was in, if it could even be called that, had a heavy metal door at the far end of the bed and a side table with water. Why was there water if she couldn't even reach it?

She heard heavy footsteps approaching, then a voice… a female crying out. *What the hell was going on?* A latch flipped down on the door, and then wild eyes came into view. They were terrifying. Bolts on the door shifted three times

The figure walked in wearing a mask, and a black silk robe. He was completely naked beneath it.

"Finally awake."

"Please. Why are you doing this?"

"Chloe."

"How do you know my name?"

He scoffed. "Oh I know a lot about you." He peeled back the covers to reveal her naked body, then covered her back up. She glimpsed at a small black tattoo of a ram, almost like the sign of Aries on his left wrist.

"Let me go, please. I won't tell anyone."

He chuckled and tucked a strand of hair behind her ear.

"Let's not talk like that." He stroked the side of her face, she wanted to bite his fingers.

"I'm thirsty."

He reached for the glass of water. "Sit up."

She struggled but managed to pull herself up partially. He leaned the glass against her dry lips and she drank. "Slow now. You'll choke."

Once she was done, he placed the glass down again. After, he took a hold of her chin and turned her face from side to side observing her before coming in close and gazing into her eyes the way an eye doctor would. She could feel his hot breath on her. It was stale and smelled like cigarette smoke.

“My wrists, they hurt.”

His eyes flared as he looked at them, then without saying another word he got up and left. Anxiety crept up in her chest when he returned a few minutes later holding a serrated edged knife.

Chapter 25

By early afternoon they were still at the crime scene.

Dark clouds had moved in threatening to empty. A cold wind blew the leaves and smaller twigs along the ground. It gave Ben an eerie feeling to think that only hours earlier the killer had been here dropping a lifeless body into the brook.

Crime scene investigation and guys from Bangor FBI were having a bit of a spat over the way things were being handled. Ben didn't want to get caught up in it, instead he decided to go and have a few words with Douglas Adams. Dakota had already warned him that the young park ranger wasn't exactly all there. He was a little slow and because of that people tended to walk over the kid.

Ben cast a glance back at officers who were now in thick yellow raincoats scouring the woods for more evidence. He took out his phone and used the video on it to capture what he could of the scene. He wanted something to look back on later that evening. He moved three hundred and sixty degrees until he had what he needed.

He had to find the connection. There was always a reason why they took them. For Henri Bruns it was the use of their bodies as living sculptures. It was a sick fantasy, but he truly believed he was giving back to the world. Instead of working with those who wanted to donate their body for medical purposes, he murdered people, stripped them of their flesh, and began his sick game of turning them into human sculptures through plastination. It was macabre but then again he was disturbing.

What was really strange about this murder site was no birds or animals could be heard. It was almost as if they sensed death and went around it. Or perhaps it was the rumble of thunder in the distance as a storm approached. They would have to work fast if they didn't want to lose any vital evidence.

"Speed it up, folks," Ben said nervously, looking up at

a gray sky. He approached Douglas with Dakota.

"Dougy, this is Benjamin Forrester, he has a few questions for you."

His eyes sunk back in his skull and he had deep black circles beneath them. He also spoke with a slight stutter.

"How can I help?"

"You've called in the deaths of the last two women. I have to ask myself — why you and not one of the other rangers? I mean there are two hundred and fifty of you in the summer period. It strikes me as a little odd."

He shrugged and got this faraway look in his eyes as if he was zoning out.

Dakota snapped her fingers in front of his face. "Dougy."

"What?"

"Answer the man."

"I don't know. I work a lot of shifts."

"But some of the areas that the women were found in were off-limits to the public because of nesting. Why would you be up in those areas?"

Again he shrugged. Ben knew that trying to extract any information from him wasn't going to be easy.

"Come, walk with me," Ben said to him. He motioned to Dakota that he wanted to go alone. They walked a short distance away.

"How long have you been doing this, Dougy?" Ben asked.

"Five years."

"You like it?"

"Oh yeah, I get to come out here and see all the birds and animals, I love it."

"Do you have a girlfriend, Dougy?"

He hesitated to reply to that so Ben continued.

"Doesn't matter. Where do you live?"

He pointed to the west.

"Tremont?"

He didn't reply again. On Mount Desert Island there were four towns, Eden, Mount Desert, Southwest Harbor, and Tremont. Each of those areas had smaller villages. Ben continued to give him a nudge in a direction.

"Which one?"

"In a cabin. I live in one of the cabins near Echo Lake."

They passed by a group of officers, Danvers looked over and scowled. Two game warden officers were having a cigarette close to the road. One of them was Ted Bishop.

"You live alone?"

"Yeah," Douglas replied.

"What do you like to do when you're not working? Got any hobbies?"

As they continued walking closer to the road, Douglas began to get all twitchy and nervous, looking like he couldn't figure out where Ben was leading him. A few cars drove by and Douglas slowed his pace. Ben motioned him on using the back of his hand on the small of his back.

"I don't have any. I work."

"Come on. You're telling me you live out in this beautiful area and all you do is work?"

He ummed and arghed. Ben glanced around as he continued walking. His eyes scanning the groups of people who were behind the police tape as well as those who were helping. Often curiosity would get the better of a serial killer. It was common to find them at the crime scene watching from a distance. They loved to return and see who was working the case. Next to taking their victims, the thrill of being within a few feet of investigators turned them on.

Ben thought of the many high-profile criminals he had visited behind bars. He went in to understand how they thought. Why they did what they had. He learned more in those years interviewing them than he ever did at the academy or on the job. It was the reason why the FBI pulled him in on some of the toughest cases. He had a way of getting underneath the skin of killers, and for the longest time it had worked until Henri. He was a completely different breed of killer. He had an understanding of psychology and used it to taunt the police.

"I hunt."

Two words but it was the beginning.

"What do you hunt?"

"Whitetail bucks, moose, and bear."

"But you can't do that in Acadia, right? Hunting and trapping are prohibited. So where do you go?"

"Vassalboro."

"Two hours' drive. That's quite a distance."

"Not really. It's quite scenic."

Ben clasped his hands behind his back and nodded slowly. A few more trucks and cars passed them until they reached the edge of the road.

"You like the hunt or the kill?"

"Bringing them home."

Ben nodded. "I bet you have quite a collection."

"Yeah…" he trailed off.

"Maybe I can come out and take a look."

"I don't know, I don't own the place."

He could see Douglas's hands shaking slightly out the corner of his eye. Earlier, Dakota had told him that

Douglas had nearly lost his job for taking medication and being found asleep behind the wheel. Another time a report had come in about him spying on a group of teens bathing. He'd denied it of course but it was enough to consider him a likely suspect.

"Hey Dougy," Ted Bishop called out to him. "Danvers wants a word with you."

"I gotta go."

"Good talking with you, Dougy. We'll chat again."

Ben watched him stroll back. Ted met him and cast a glance over his shoulder at Ben. Dakota walked over.

"So any luck with the birdman of Alcatraz?"

He shook his head. "What's the deal between Dougy and Ted Bishop?"

"Ah, he's like Ted's shadow. He wanted to follow in his footsteps but didn't get hired by the Maine Warden Service."

"Where's Ted live?"

"Locally. In town. Eden."

"Any word from officers on interviews done with other

park rangers?"

"Nothing so far. You really think it's a park ranger?"

"Two women disappear every summer. There are eighty park rangers, that number swells to two hundred and fifty in the summer. What happens to the other one hundred and seventy after the summer?"

"It's usually part-time work or they return to other national parks in the area. They go where the need is."

"So it's possible that someone could do the killings then leave again. Might explain why they only occur in the summer."

"Maybe. Then again the winters here are brutal. No one is going to want to be in those woods in the winter."

"Perhaps that's why he keeps a few, to tide him over until the following summer. I want the addresses of both Douglas and Ted."

"Ben, you're going to need a warrant if you want to search their residence."

"Then let's make it happen."

A light rain began to fall. Within an hour it had

turned into a heavy downpour. What little hope they had of retaining evidence would likely be washed away. That was the challenge of dealing with cases on the coast. In a moment's notice the weather could change and you could be dealing with gale force winds coming off the North Atlantic Ocean, and rain that soaked you to the bone. Every hour that passed ate away at Ben's insides.

When his phone rang again Ben was seeking shelter under a tree with another group of officers. The body had been taken to the medical examiner's office. They would soon have a clearer idea of how she died. He jabbed accept on the phone call. The sound of Henri's voice only chewed him up more.

"Found another, haven't you, Ben?"

Ben clenched his jaw. "What do you want?"

"Let's talk."

Chapter 26

He studied Dr. Benjamin Forrester from a distance. He'd never had an FBI agent on his tail before. The police sure, but they were chumps and barely capable of doing their own job. But he'd read about Forrester. The man who profiled serial killers and caught the best of them and now he was hunting him.

It was amusing to watch them chase their tails as they tried to join the dots and piece together how he operated. There was something sexually arousing about it all. Outwitting, outsmarting, and staying one step ahead of them gave him a great deal of pleasure.

He knew all about Forrester. His background, his loss, and his obsession with catching Skinner. Now there was a killer who had earned his respect. If anyone had proven they were capable of eluding the cops, it was him.

Oh, how he missed seeing the reports on the news about his latest victim, or the case they had been building.

He'd read through Forrester's book. Why did he write it? He must have thought he was so smart revealing how he had outwitted those he caught, but had he realized he had revealed how to avoid being detected?

That's why this worked so well.

Forrester's book was one among many books he had read. Long before he started taking women he had studied how Dahmer, Bundy, Gacy, the Green River Killer, and many others had been caught. It always came down to a few mistakes. Letting a victim escape, killing prostitutes, sticking to one method of taking them. They were all idiots. But not him. He was going to follow in the footsteps of Skinner and remain uncaught.

Behind the yellow tape he watched as Ben spoke on the phone. He looked distraught, a mere shell of a man that was clinging to past successes. He must have thought he was a big shot telling others what to do when he had no clue. He wasn't close to catching him. His questions were leading nowhere except to the death of his own daughter.

Chloe, she was a sweet one. He couldn't see a resemblance of her in Forrester's face. She must have looked more like her mother. He chuckled to himself thinking about how Skinner had taken the life of Forrester's wife and son. You play with the bull you get the horns.

Skinner was a master at it. He had set the bar high, but it was one that he was more than prepared to meet. Of course this meant having his own reasons for killing, his own unique style. Something that would set him apart from the others and make him go down in history as one of the best, or in their minds, worst serial killers that Maine had seen.

He was tempted to go up and speak to him, ask him for his autograph. He played it out in his mind. "Dr. Forrester, could I get an autograph?" he would mumble as he handed him his book. "Can you make it out to Chloe, my mother?" Oh to peer into his eyes as he heard his daughter's name.

Keeping his eyes fixed on him, he walked parallel to

him as Forrester went over to that bitch Dakota. Now there was a woman he had considered taking. How easy it would be. He'd sat many a night outside her home watching her. A quick shot from the Taser and she wouldn't be able to go for her gun. What a rush that would be! His eyes surveyed the numerous police and FBI milling around with their hands in their pockets. *That's it, keep it up, you idiots.* He couldn't believe people paid these imbeciles to catch someone of his artistic talent. For all their studying and droning on about how they had caught serial killers, they still weren't even close to nabbing him. Maybe he would send them a note. Give them a little teaser of what was about to come. Help them. Help? Did he really want to help them catch him? But that was it. The thrill wasn't in taking the women or keeping them for his own purposes, neither was it the excitement of getting away with it. He'd thought long and hard about this. It was the exhilaration of nearly getting caught. Every time they had got close, he felt the rush. *So go ahead, try to catch me. You won't!*

Chapter 27

Chloe's hands and feet were finally free. She blinked hard coming out of the coma-like state. What was he using? She was so groggy and barely able to keep her eyes open. But she had to, she had to get out of here.

There'd only ever been one time she recalled being this badly drugged, and that was a year ago when she had some alcohol and completely forgot that she'd taken medication earlier that day. It felt like a weight crushing down on her. The fear of falling asleep and never waking up kept her blinking hard. She rolled off the bed onto the hard floor completely naked. He hadn't left anything on her. Where were her clothes?

She reached for the glass of water on the side table. Her vision doubled as her hand reached and then knocked it over. Water trickled over the edge. She patted it with her hands and brought it to her face, allowing the cold and wet to shock her multiple times. She needed to stay awake.

Her eyes fell on a mound beneath the bed. What was that? She reached under, raking the granite stone with her fingers until she caught hold of material. It was a pair of jeans. She hadn't worn jeans, had she? Her memory was sketchy. Her eyes opened and shut as whatever he had given her tried to force her back into a slumber.

Her vision doubled then corrected itself.

She fell hard against the bed trying to get back into the jeans. Unable, she tossed them to one side and stumbled around the room like a penned animal. It wasn't a room but a torture chamber with chains that hung loosely at the far side. Below that, a pool of dry blood. This was worse than any prison. Who had been in here before? One of the women they had found dead?

The granite was harsh and cold against her feet. She staggered over to the metal door and fell against it before tugging at the handle. To her surprise it opened. She tried to recall what had happened, but the drugs fragmented her mind. Had he forgotten to lock it? Was he still here?

How much time had passed since she last woke up? Peering out of the cell she found the outside to look even more frightening. It was dark and dingy. A musty smell stung her nostrils.

Were these mining tunnels?

Wherever she was it wasn't a place that had been used in a long time. Small dim lights flickered above her. The strained sound of sobbing could be heard throughout. Music? Like a symphony orchestra it was low and barely audible.

She rubbed her side, which throbbed after falling against the bed. A cool wind howled and nipped at her skin. All she could see were multiple doors to other rooms. All of them were the same as hers. A thick, heavy metal with bolts on the outside.

She moved along the tunnel, keeping her back pushed against it. There was no way of knowing where he was or what he would do if he caught her. She palmed her head, trying to push back the pain of a headache.

Where was she? Could this be a basement? No, it

couldn't be, there was water seeping down the stone.

She kept moving towards a glimmer of light farther down the tunnel. She desperately wanted to run but without any shoes, not knowing where she was, and feeling groggy, it was too dangerous. Suddenly she gripped the stone wall and vomited. It came out hard. The stomach acid burned her throat.

The closer she got to the room with the light, the more fearful she became. Rounding the corner, she found herself in a small room with a table and chair. Her captor wasn't there but masks were. *He was wearing a mask.* There were two on the side of the table, old and wrinkly, makeup to the left of that, and animal heads all over the walls. *I've got to find something, anything to defend myself,* she thought. Her vision doubled again and her head dropped. Stay awake. She reached out for the table to steady her. Her hands groped for anything that could be used as a weapon. On the side was a pair of scissors. Small, like the kind that was used to cut hair. She snatched them up and staggered backwards. Her body fell hard against a wooden door. The door swung open and she landed flat on her ass. Twisting around, she peered into the darkness.

"Hello?" she muttered, seeing what she thought were people. Darkness crept in at the sides of her eyes. No, no, I must stay awake, she told herself.

Pushing up on her elbows, then her palms, she staggered to her feet and leaned against the wall. It was wet and reeked of a smell so putrid it made her want to be sick again. She ran her hand up the stone looking for a light switch, then back and forth in front of her in the darkness until she caught hold of a string. As soon as she yanked it, she thought she was in hell.

All around her were human bodies in various stages of decomposition. *Oh my god.* Her eyes fixed on the back of one of them. The skin was brown and haggard as if it had aged and dried up. From the neck down to the butt cheeks the flesh had been slashed and sewn together. Pieces of stuffing spilled out the seam. In some of them was wood shavings, in others a precast urethane mold. It was human taxidermy. Gasping for air and stumbling backwards she fell against one, its stiff hand touched her skin. Collapsing, two of the bodies toppled onto her. Their dead eyes peered into hers. It was a grisly sight that she wasn't prepared for. You could never be prepared for this. She fought her way out from underneath the mutilated corpses. There had to have been at least thirty bodies, most didn't even resemble humans anymore. The skin had changed. She squeezed her eyes shut, pushing the horror from her mind.

As she tried to make her way back to the door, the full effect of whatever he had given her was overwhelming. She could barely stay awake, let alone stand.

A noise from behind startled her. Standing in the doorway was a figure — the one in the old man's mask. Chloe, scared for her life, backed up fast holding out the scissors.

"Get back. I will kill you if you come near me."

"I see you've found my prized possessions. Aren't they beautiful?"

"You sick fucker, get back."

He moved towards her and bounced from side to side as if he was about to play a game of tag.

"Where are you going to go, Chloe? There is nowhere to run."

Her vision blurred, creating multiple versions of him in front of her. She slashed the air, desperate to keep him at a distance. There was no way in hell she would let him perform taxidermy on her. Her heart was pounding in her chest. She had never felt so much fear.

"Come on now. Drop the scissors and I won't punish you."

"Stay back," she said, continuing to jab and swipe in front of her. The world at the corners of her eyes was fading to black. *No, stay awake!* He laughed as if he could tell she was fighting the effects of the injection he'd given her.

Chloe pounced towards the opening but was too slow. He slammed one of the bodies into her, knocking her down and causing the scissors to slip across the ground.

She scrambled forward. Pain coursed through her body. The world began to cave in on her.

"Shit. You've grazed yourself. Now look what you've done."

She couldn't keep her eyes open any longer.

"That's a girl. Go to sleep. Sleep."

The last image was of him crouching over her. A sick and twisted face inches away from her own.

Chapter 28

There were no easy ways to find answers. Police banged on doors, interviewed families of victims, and followed up on any tips that came in to the joint task force. It was a slow and painful process that was only made worse by every passing day and the occasional nutcase who wanted to waste police time with a false confession.

Ben was reminded of what his instructor had told him back at the academy.

"It's hours of sheer frustration followed by moments of pure terror."

That was the reality.

After an abrupt phone call from Henri Bruns in which he hung up, Ben spent a good portion of that afternoon with Patricia Welling's family. Victim's services had been with them since they came down to the medical examiner's office and identified her body.

It was learned that Patricia had left one Sunday morning three years ago, saying she was going to hike up Cadillac Mountain. It was the tallest peak on Mount Desert Island. At an elevation of one thousand five hundred and twenty-eight feet above sea level you could see above the clouds. Her last words were, "I'll be back this evening."

She was never seen again. Her mother had been devastated by the whole ordeal. The recent news of her body being found didn't bring her any more relief. While victim's families were usually glad to have the body returned so they could have a proper burial, the thought of what happened, haunted them.

The profile Ben had created so far of the perpetrator was based on the girls being from out of town but this one wasn't. Which was leading him to believe that the killer wasn't choosing them randomly. Or was he? These seemed like opportunist kidnappings. He wasn't stalking them in the way other serial killers would follow their victims for weeks or even months. He wasn't studying what they did, or who was with them. Instead they were walking into his territory the way a gazelle would stroll through tall reeds unaware that a lion lay in wait. Or could it be something else? Was he basing his selection on something that the women had in common? But what was it?

It struck him he hadn't thought about Jake Ashton, Earl's son. He didn't think for a moment that he had anything to do with this. The kid had no fight in him. He was scared when Ben pulled him from the car. But maybe he could provide some insights into what Chloe might have told him.

* * *

Dakota made contact with Jake as she was certain Earl wouldn't have given Ben the time of day. To ensure that he didn't bolt, Dakota asked him to meet down by the harbor. It was meant to feel informal — a simple follow-up on the charges they had wanted to press against Ben.

Dakota headed for the harbor late that afternoon. It was a short ten-minute ride. Along the way she called her lawyer who was handling some issues with her ex, Michael, who had recently returned to the town hoping to patch things up. She'd told him in no uncertain terms that it was over. He'd made that painfully obvious the moment he chose to screw around.

There were lots of lobster boats in the harbor that afternoon. Most of the fishermen were busy cleaning their traps and nets. Among the eight cars in the lot was Jake's 2003 Pontiac. It was parked at an angle and idling in the rain. She pulled up beside him and could hear rock music blaring from his woofer speakers. She gestured for him to get in. He had this look on his face as if he was tired of dealing with cops.

Outside, the wind could be heard rattling the wire grid railing that went along the dock. The door opened, and he hopped into the passenger side.

"Jake," Dakota said.

"What's this about?"

"You knew Chloe well."

"Somewhat."

"Do you know anything about her disappearance?"

He didn't even hesitate, he just shook his head. "Nope."

She looked out the window at the sun, which was trying to break through dark clouds. The sound of a bell ringing gently in the wind could be heard every few minutes.

Jake looked rugged and athletic like any typical high school kid who played sports. He tapped his fingers on his jeans nervously.

"So?" he asked.

"Did Chloe ever tell you that she felt as if she was being watched or do you know anyone who might have wanted to hurt her?"

He shook his head. "Do you mind if I smoke?"

"No, go ahead."

He pulled a pack of Marlboro Lights out, tapped one out, and placed it between his lips. Dakota, who was still trying to kick the habit herself, flipped the top on her old lighter. The end of his cigarette glowed orange and hissed as he took a few hard pulls on it. He touched the button to bring the window down just slightly. Wafts of smoke drifted out and vanished.

"So are you close to catching this guy?"

"What makes you think it's a guy?"

"Really?" he shook his head as if he was the smart one. Dakota knew a lot of the kids in town. It wasn't a big place. She saw the same faces every day on the way to work, and knew who the repeat offenders were — those who did graffiti, poached, and got up to general mischief. Mainly it was damage to property and trespassing. Minor stuff, but it got annoying after a while. Jake liked to talk big, but he never stepped over the line until Chloe came along. His old man, Earl, wouldn't let him get away with it. Earl was a fisherman. A no-nonsense individual who drank hard and spent most of his time out on his 1970 red-and-white, thirty-four-foot lobster boat.

"Where were you Saturday night?"

"Having a few beers with friends. Jason Whittling can confirm it."

"What about your father?"

"Asleep at home, at least he was when I left there."

"Okay," Dakota said while staring out at the bay.

"I thought you said this was about the charges?"

"Yeah, yeah it is."

"Well?"

"No charges are going to be laid against you."

He straightened up in the seat. "Against me? He was the one who tossed me out."

Dakota scratched the side of her nose. "I think we both know what happened, Jake. So let's just cut to the chase here. I'm going to give you a word of advice. Drop it. He could easily have filed charges against you."

His face went red. "I didn't do anything."

"Well I'm sure Chloe might have something different to say on the matter."

He let out a slight chuckle. "That's going to be a little difficult now, isn't it?"

She cast a sideways glance and narrowed her eyes.

"If I find out that you were in any way connected with

Chloe's disappearance, so help me God I will make sure you spend the rest of your young life behind bars."

"Yes, ma'am," he said sarcastically.

It was something she'd never get used to in Eden Falls. Youngsters didn't take the police seriously. Maybe because it was a tight-knit community and a number of the parents were on the town council. If you ruffled their feathers, you heard about it. It was one of the reasons why Chief Danvers rode them so hard. Unless it was drastic, they had the discretion to let things slide. Problem was, he let one too many things slide in this town.

Jake stared blankly at her.

"Can I go?"

She nodded.

Dakota stared out of her windshield at him as he came around the front of the car. Between raindrops coming down hard she could have sworn he smirked. He took his time, gave a nod, and hopped back into his car. The music blared, causing her car to vibrate again. A few more seconds and he was gone. It took everything she had to keep from losing her cool. Memories of arguments with Michael bombarded her. Some men weren't meant to be with women.

She turned over the ignition and reversed out. The car crawled up the steep incline that led down to the harbor. Chewing over her conversation, she lingered behind a stop sign for a few minutes before someone startled her by honking a horn.

Chapter 29

Always dealing with red tape. Ben was sick of it. He wanted to burst into Douglas Adams's home and search it immediately but that wasn't how it was done. They needed a stronger reason to search his cabin than he acted like a weirdo and liked to hunt. Half of the population of Maine were hunters, at least that was Chief Danvers's excuse. Of course it was an exaggeration, but he had a point.

Ben returned home that evening frustrated by the lack of decent leads. They now had two dead bodies, two missing girls, and a smidgen of insight from the medical examiner's report.

It didn't help that a reporter from the Henri Bruns case had shown up in town. Edwin Parker was a sleazy reporter who would do anything for a story. He had been arrested for breaking and entering into Ben's home after the death of his wife and son. There were no lengths this man wasn't prepared to go to in order to dig up dirt.

The headline of the tabloid called *The Eagle* was "Renowned FBI Agent Fails to Catch Serial Killer."

He wasn't bothered by the title, it was the photos that he'd stolen from his home and published without permission that pissed him off. The lawyers had a field day with him and the tabloid company tossed him out on his ear. Now some would think that he would have given up but after serving some time he was back out and back to his old tricks. This time however it was with a completely different tabloid.

It made him sick to his stomach.

Ben poured himself a scotch and tried to convince himself that he was doing all he could to find her. He now understood what it was like for parents with a missing child. The utter despair and the sense of guilt. That you hadn't done enough. That you could do more. His mind was constantly being bombarded.

The next time his phone rang he didn't answer it. He wasn't going to get into a game with that lunatic. He wanted Ben to believe he could help catch him. But that was just a lie, a means to taunt him. The FBI had run a trace on the call but Bruns had used some type of routing system that forwarded the calls to an internet café where he was using VOIP software to phone. They had managed to track down two of the cafes but none of them had surveillance. You had to be more than smart to catch these types of killers. Most of the time it required a great deal of luck.

His eyelids were heavy. Sitting in his chair with the Glock 22 beside him, all he wanted to do was get out there and shoot the bastard that had taken his daughter.

For years he had caught these creeps and the justice system had locked them up but that wasn't justice. Nor was offering them forgiveness for their crimes. He wanted them to pay. He wanted to see them suffer the way their victims had.

He wasn't sure when he fell asleep but again his dreams were filled with the terror of losing Elizabeth and Adam. This time, however, when he saw them in his dream Elizabeth spoke to him. She blamed him for not watching over Chloe.

When Ben's eyelids snapped open, he found himself gasping for air. He took another drink to steady his nerves. His phone showed four messages. He knew they were from him. Nate told him to change the phone number, but he knew he would find the next one. That's what kept him ahead of the law. His ability to outsmart the police.

Sitting in the sunroom at night there was a sense that he was being watched. He grabbed his .40 and moved towards the window and gazed out. It was dark outside but he could see the moon's reflection on the water. He moved to the back door and opened it. The sound of waves lapping against the shore and animals rustling in the surrounding forest was all that could be heard.

He was about to go back inside when he caught out the side of his eye a figure moving between the trees. It was subtle at first. But then the moon's light reflected off them.

Ben turned sharply and ran towards the tree line. The figure bolted, and he gave chase. Pushing his way through thick undergrowth he saw the silhouette darting in and out.

He raised his weapon. "Stop, I'll shoot."

They weren't going to stop. He considered firing for a second but without knowing who it was or why they were there, he lowered the Glock. It wasn't like in the movies where you could just randomly shoot at anyone. Every time that gun was pulled, papers had to be filled out, and an explanation had to be given as to why. And god forbid if you fired and someone was hit. They would take your badge and gun and treat you like a criminal. It then became a matter of whether you were justified in using force.

Eventually he made his way back. They knew these woods better than him. It was like they had just vanished into thin air. Had he imagined it? He had been taking headache medication and drinking. It was possible that the alcohol was playing tricks on him.

Could it have been Bruns? The thought that he was watching him from a distance sent a shiver up his spine. It wasn't that he was afraid of him, he was afraid of what he might do if he ever got his hands on Bruns before anyone else did.

He'd chewed over scenarios in his head for the past two years but it only pained him. There was nothing that could be done. Bruns wanted him to feel the pain, to be reminded every day that he had lost and Bruns had escaped. It was all a game to him. Nothing more.

As he trudged back towards the house feeling defeated, his phone buzzed. This time it was an email with an attachment. He clicked it to see who it was from, a second passed and then a photo came up on his screen. He felt his stomach sink.

Chapter 30

Nate had taken away his phone to get them to trace where the sick photo had come from.

"It's him, isn't it?"

"We don't know that."

"Bullshit! Of course we do, Nate. He's back to finish off what he started. All of this was just a game. He's been playing games from the start trying to make us think that it's someone else but it's him. He's got Chloe and I'm not going to see her alive again."

It was just after ten in the morning. Nate and several of the agents from Bangor FBI were at his house. Some of the local officers were out in the woods searching for anything that might have been dropped by the visitor in the night. Dakota was chatting to the chief.

"All we know right now is that he figured out your phone number and he saw what was released in the media."

"That photo must have come from the same place that he was sending me phone calls from. Tell me, how else could he get hold of that photo?"

"Maybe he's in contact with whoever is behind these murders, or perhaps that photo didn't come from him."

The frustration and tension in the home was high that morning. The photo was a clear shot of Chloe with her eyes closed, on a bed. There was no way of knowing if she was alive or dead. Her mouth was bound with a cloth, and her wrists zip tied to posts. The top half of her was naked. Whoever sent it was making a statement. This wasn't taunting, it was about driving home a message that he was in control. He was the one who had the power to kill her or keep her alive. That's why another body had been found. He wanted to let the police know that whether they were investigating this case or not, he would still go about his work.

He was above them, uncatchable. Or perhaps he wanted to be caught. It wouldn't have been the first time that a serial killer had left behind messages. Some were clear. Blood on a wall that said, "Catch me please, I can't stop killing." Others were less obvious. It was like they were fighting a war inside themselves — between that which they knew was right and the demon that drove them on.

While the storm had subsided, and the sky was clearer, a storm was still raging inside of Ben. As much as he was trying to keep it under control, it was becoming even more difficult.

Ben went upstairs to get away from the noise of police, phone calls being made, and investigators arguing over the implications of this on the community. Who gave a damn about the community, at this rate there wouldn't be one left. It had already been torn apart as the public started pointing the finger at the police's inability to do their job.

Inside of Chloe's room, Ben could see officers scouring the forest. They weren't going to find anything. If this was Bruns he wouldn't be that stupid. He cast a glance around the room. It was still the way she had left it. The bed unmade, her guitar on the side, a stack of mystery books on a shelf, and her sparring gloves. He couldn't fight back the tears any longer. He was a father first, then a detective. He grabbed a few tissues from a side table and wiped his face.

He picked up one of the gloves.

"Fight, Chloe," he muttered.

Chapter 31

Curled up in a ball on the bed, fading in and out of consciousness, she could hear another voice. A different one this time. Two men were arguing. She couldn't make out what it was they were saying but one of them was impatient. She groaned as she sat up. The first thing she noticed was her hands and feet weren't bound this time.

Then like an out of focus picture the room snapped back into view. At the same time she began to comprehend what they were saying.

"You unbolted that door. You are the one responsible for the other girl getting out."

"It was a mistake. It won't happen again."

She couldn't tell if it was one person changing their voice or two people.

"I know it won't happen again because if it does, it will be your body that they find next. Do I make myself clear, you imbecile?"

"Uh-huh."

"Now get back to work."

There was silence and then the sounds of footsteps outside. A few bolts being unlocked across the way. A plate dropped on the floor. She went through the cycle of what she had heard since being taken. If she wasn't drugged up she would get two, maybe three visits a day. The person always wore a mask but she was sure that there were two of them. One of them appeared shorter than the other.

She listened carefully as the man did his rounds. She heard another voice, this time a woman's. She was petrified. Possibly new? Chloe hadn't seen them but she was certain there were at least three other women in the rooms. One of them had screamed and fought when he went into her cell. Her cries were soon quieted. Now all she heard were sobs. He broke them down. How? She wasn't sure. Maybe he took away their food or raped them. She wasn't sure if she had been raped. She had felt hands on her but nothing more. What were they waiting for?

A metal bolt clunked, and the door opened up. With a face covered up by the mask, the man entered holding a plate with a sandwich on it and a glass of water. The mask had scared her at first. It was distorted and twisted under the influence of the drugs but now without feeling heavy she could see clearly.

The man turned without saying a word.

"Please. Stay," Chloe said.

He cast a glance over his shoulder.

"You're not him, are you?" she said. On the outside he looked the same. He was a similar build but a different height. "You unbolted the door, didn't you?"

He never replied, just stared at her. She could tell he was looking at her body, which was partially covered with a sheet.

"It's okay, you can come closer."

He shuffled across the room until he was near to her.

"Do you have to wear that mask?"

He nodded slowly. There was something very odd

about him but at the same time she could sense that he was different to the one that had caught her trying to escape. The other man was brutal and showed no mercy. But this one. Maybe she could reach him.

"Please. Can you help me get out of here?"

He shook his head and then went to leave.

"I'm sorry. Don't go," she said.

The man paused at the door, his hand on the lock, before deciding to return.

"What's your name?" she asked, taking a bite of her food. It was just ham, but she hadn't eaten in a while and her stomach was grumbling and aching to be fed. Of course he wouldn't tell her his name. She noticed he was looking at her breasts. His head swept back and forth over her. His eyes, round and dark brown, seemed to penetrate her from beyond the mask.

"Do you like them?" she said, placing the plate down and pulling back the covers to expose herself even more. She could see his chest rising and falling a little faster and heard him swallow hard.

"You can touch them if you want."

He shifted back in his seat and shot a glance at the door nervously.

"Go on."

She reached for his hand but he pulled it back fast then ran it around the back of his neck. He shook his head and stood up and began walking around the room as though trying to determine what he should be doing.

"It's okay," she said, uncovering herself some more until he got a good look at her naked body. She reached out again for his left hand as he passed by and this time he didn't pull away. She placed it on her left breast. His hand was cold. Her nipple hardened beneath it.

"See, it's okay."

His other hand came forward, and he touched the other breast and began pawing them greedily. She could tell it was turning him on and that was exactly what she wanted.

"Do you want me?" she asked.

He nodded, rocking back and forth like a psychotic

patient who was off his medication.

She tugged at his arm until he was on top straddling her. He reached down his head and began nuzzling his face between her breasts. It repulsed her but she allowed it. She could feel his tongue slipping out of the opening on the mask. While he feasted on her, she slipped one hand over to the side and took a firm hold of the glass. He was sucking away at her when she brought the glass down hard on the back of his head with as much force as she could. It smashed and a shard cut into her hand. One swift knee to the groin and she pushed him off her and slid out. Crouched on the floor, she snatched up a piece of the glass, expecting him to put up a fight. The edge was jagged and pointed at one end. She didn't think about clothes. All that pushed through her mind was to get out of there.

Go, go now, move it.

Moving like a mountain lion she sprang forward but before she left the room, she glanced back at the now unconscious figure. Who was it? Did he have a key on him?

There was no point in running if she couldn't get out. She moved over to him and started feeling around in his pockets. There was nothing there except a wallet. She pulled it out and glanced at the ID. *Douglas Adams, Park Ranger.*

A park ranger! What the hell? She dropped it, whimpering and backing up to escape. She dashed out of the room and turned left towards where she'd heard the men's voices coming from. She moved fast across the granite floor and dashed down the tunnel. There had to be a way out, she was sure of it. Perhaps there wasn't a key to get out. She kept moving until she saw a wooden ladder in the distance at the far end of the tunnel. Above it a speck of light illuminated the foot of the ladder.

In a frenzied haste she bolted past the room that had the masks and bodies hung up. She didn't stop to see if there was anyone in there.

As soon as she placed a foot on the rung of the ladder she began climbing two at a time. Scrambling up towards the light above, all she wanted was to escape. She was so close to her freedom that she could feel hope inside her increasing with every step she took. Her heart felt like it was about to burst out of her chest as she got closer to the top.

The moment her head came out she felt a hand grip her by the throat. Out the corner of her eye she saw him. As she gasped and struggled, he lifted her out of the hole by his bare hands. Now in the grasp of her captor, she flailed around as he began strangling her in midair. Her feet dangled a few inches off the floor as he slammed her up against the wall. His grotesque mask came close. She felt his hot breath on her face.

"I thought you were different." Her eyes took in what she was seeing. She was inside a cabin. Animal heads everywhere. She still had the shard of glass in her hand but with him choking her she was about to lose consciousness any minute now.

Chloe thought fast, she jammed the shard of glass into his outstretched arm. He shrieked with pain and dropped her. Coughing and spluttering, she began crawling on her hands and knees away from him like an injured animal.

She didn't even look behind her to see him pulling the glass from his arm.

"Where do you think you're going?"

She screamed as he came up behind her and grabbed hold of her by the hair and yanked her upright. He clamped one arm around her throat and slammed her down onto the floor. Now with all his weight he pressed down on her chest with his knee and began choking her with both hands. Oh god, he was going to kill her now. This wasn't the way it was meant to end. Chloe began to see stars; everything was beginning to turn black.

Desperation overtook her as she drove a knee into his side but it did nothing. It only angered him more and made him squeeze harder.

Gasping for air, she stared into the eye sockets of his mask. Pure evil stared back.

"Die, bitch!"

She raked at his jacket with her fingers and then

clawed at his mask but it was no use, he was too heavy and much stronger than her. Suddenly, she felt air flood her lungs as the man collapsed on top of her. Wheezing and trying to suck in as much air as she could, she felt his body slide away from her. Standing above was Douglas Adams holding a shovel.

He stared absently at the unconscious man's body. Chloe pulled herself up to a kneeling position. Sucking in more air she looked over at the man who still had his mask on.

"Thank you," she said before turning away, only to feel the full force of a shovel hit the side of her skull.

Chapter 32

Ben had divided the majority of the day between talking with the medical examiner's office and trying to figure out why he had killed again. The toxicology report came back the same as the Taylor girl. There was something that wasn't adding up about it. It was a mixture of organization and disorganization. It was uncommon for serial killers. They were usually one or the other. Either he was trying to confuse them or there were two people involved. He'd been sitting at a desk down at the local police station for the past hour, drinking a horrendous amount of bad coffee and working through the reports, when Dakota pulled up a chair.

"Good news, I think we've got a lead," Dakota said.

"How so?"

"The boys did a check on taxidermists in the area who still use formaldehyde and glycerin as a means of preserving. Seems that most use a product called Masters

Blend. Only a few use the old method of formaldehyde and glycerin."

She paused to glance down at a piece of paper in her hand.

"One to be exact — Eden-Ridge Taxidermy on the west side."

"Well, let's go."

Ben grabbed his jacket off the back of the chair and they rushed over to Eden-Ridge Taxidermy, turning west on Route 233 then south on Route 102 into Tremont. The road wound its way through the park's tall green pines. Along the way they passed several seafood restaurants and gift stores that led up to Southwest Harbor.

"Don't you think they would just order it themselves online?"

"Not unless they want to leave a trail. They are probably paying for it in cash, if they're smart."

They had finally located the store. An obscure wooden sign outside had a few of the letters missing. From the moment they stepped inside, the creepiness level went up a few notches with mounted animal heads, deer skulls, and fur skins covering every inch of space. The place wasn't much more than a wooden shack on the outskirts of town. It smelled like roadkill, and salt with a chemical odor.

Two men were huddled around a large desk, rubbing salt into the flesh side of a hide. Both of them looked like they had just stepped out of the wilderness. One of them had a thick black beard and was wearing a plaid shirt. The other was skinny, he had a sunken face and was twitching from the moment he saw them enter.

"Can I help you?"

Ben didn't waste any time getting to it. "You guys use formaldehyde and glycerin to preserve?"

"Yeah."

He asked them where they were on the night Chloe went missing and when the bodies of Rachael Taylor and other girl were found.

"At the Thirsty Whale Tavern all evening then down

at Earl Ashton's boat."

"Earl?"

Dakota made a note to follow up on that.

"Do you sell product to anyone interested in doing taxidermy themselves?"

"Nope."

Ben caught something in the way they looked at each other.

"Has anyone been in requesting if you can get them a large amount of formaldehyde and glycerin?"

They looked at each other again. The one with the beard shrugged. "Not around here."

"Well, thanks for your time," Ben turned and walked out. As they made it back to the car, Dakota kept giving him a strange look as she pulled out her phone to place a call to the Thirsty Whale Tavern.

"Hey, I'll be back in a second," he said.

She slipped into the car, speaking to the owner on the phone. Ben tossed his jacket in the vehicle and went back into the taxidermist's store. Five minutes later he came out shaking a receipt in his hand and had a name on his lips. He slipped into the car and she turned over the ignition with a frown on her face.

"How did? —"

"You don't want to know," he replied, rubbing his swollen knuckles.

"Ben."

"Just drive. I think we've got that warrant."

Chapter 33

Chloe awoke to a cold, rough feeling on the side of her face. She was lying on a wooden floor. Her head was pounding and hurt like crazy. She cried out from shock and feeling disoriented like a child waking up from surgery. A shuffle of feet behind caused her to twist.

He was sitting at a desk with his back turned. “Don’t try anything stupid, I’m not going to hurt you.” He swiveled in his chair and had a magnifying glass headset on, making one of his eyes appear bigger than the other. On the desk in front of him was a stuffed raccoon; he was in the process of pushing a black almond eye into the eye socket.

She rubbed the side of her head, wincing in pain.

“Sorry about that,” he stuttered. “But I couldn’t have you see where you were going.”

“Where am I?”

“My home.”

She took in her surroundings. A few small windows let in the remaining afternoon light. Thick metal foundational pillars held up the floor above. She gazed up and saw planks of wood. She was in a basement. He observed her as she looked around.

"Oh, I took it upon myself to redress you."

That's when she noticed she was wearing jeans and a shirt. They didn't belong to her. That bothered her even more. As she moved, she felt metal teeth cut into her leg. He'd handcuffed her to a post by her ankle. She tugged on it.

"What the hell?"

"That's for my security."

Chloe looked at him with skeptical eyes before he rubbed the back of his head.

"That was quite a knock you gave me," he muttered.

"Where is he?"

His eyes dropped. "Yeah, him." Something about the mention of his vicious partner in crime seemed to make him crawl back into the shell of who he was when the other one was around. He swiveled on the chair and went back to working on the raccoon.

"Are you going to let me go?"

"I haven't quite decided yet."

"I won't tell anyone," she said softly.

He snorted with his back turned. "I somehow doubt that."

Chloe scanned the ground for anything she could use as a weapon: a broken chunk of concrete was within a few feet but she was certain it was out of reach. Tools were hung up on the wall — a wrench, screwdrivers, and a drill.

"Why did you help me?"

"What makes you think I helped you?"

"He's not here, is he?"

He paused, holding a dark eye between his fingers.

"No, but oh he's going to be so pissed."

"Let me go please. I have a family."

He continued working away, oblivious to her pleading. She thought he would show sympathy because he had stopped the other from killing her.

"How many women have you killed?"

"I don't kill them, he does. I just bring them in."

"But he brutalizes and murders them."

His head rocked up and down, acknowledging what she was saying.

"Not all of them. The special ones are transformed. You're special, Chloe. I guess that's why I didn't let him kill you."

"Who is he?"

He let out a stifled chuckle as if he was privy to some inside joke.

"How do you like my collection?" His shift in topic was disturbing. "I've always been fond of the squirrels and raccoons. This one here and that one over there. They are so much easier to transform."

She let out a sigh and tugged at the silver handcuffs. "How long are you going to keep me here?"

"Tell me, what would you like to eat tonight?"

"What?"

"Well, I'm guessing you're hungry and thirsty. You eat, do you not?"

"Let me out of here."

"In time."

"Now," she demanded. "Let me out of here, you psycho fuck."

"Now that's not polite, Chloe. No, we won't be having any of that."

She spat at him. He tilted his head to one side and smirked. "Um, you really are beautiful when you're angry. Here," he twisted around and pulled a can of lemonade from a box and tossed it to her. "Drink."

"Drink it yourself," she slammed it back at him.

He laughed, watching the can roll on the ground near his feet. Taking in a deep breath, he turned and switched on the radio. Symphony music began to play, and he went back to work on the unfortunate creature.

"Let me out," she screamed a few times, but he just turned up the volume.

Chapter 34

A few hours later, after getting a search warrant from the county judge, the joint task force was gearing up to raid the house of Douglas Adams. The chief believed it to be a little excessive, but Ben didn't. If they were right, they weren't going to take any chances. Ben checked the ammo in his Glock before pushing it into his holster underneath his jacket.

It was a fast drive over to Echo Lake on the west side of Mount Desert Island. Douglas's cabin was nestled in the heart of the woods. Barely visible from the road, eight blue-and-white cruisers parked haphazardly in front of the small, dank-looking cabin. The clapboards were weathered and looked as if they had seen better days. The roof had been patched up and a steel chimney stuck out the side like a flexed arm. After they bailed out, the ten-man SWAT team immediately jumped into action. Officers set up a perimeter around the place.

The lot was overgrown with weeds. A brick well filled in with soil was off to one side. It looked as if he had attempted to build a fence around the area. The posts were in but no more than that.

With adrenaline pumping, Ben was eager to get inside but the commander of the unit told him to hang back while they approached the cabin. They were better trained for this. Even though he had worked as a sniper back in the day he didn't want to screw this up. Waiting for their signal, he hung back behind a black SWAT truck. Dakota had her piece drawn; all of them were ready for the worst-case scenario.

You didn't negotiate with these type of people, they would kill their victims and themselves long before SWAT entered. The only way to get them was to catch them off guard. The chief had already called ahead to the ranger's station to make sure he wasn't on duty.

Best case, they entered and he wasn't there but the women were; worst case, he'd killed them already. At this point Ben was just pleased they had something to go on.

Days of frustration had begun to take its toll on all of them.

The SWAT team took up a linear style formation and began moving in soundlessly with assault rifles on the ready. The house was about twenty feet from the driveway. The one at the front was carrying a ballistic shield. Another one of them had a battering ram.

Ben saw them pat each other on the shoulder and they positioned themselves to the side of the front door. The first one banged it and shouted... *Police Department, Search Warrant.*

Then all hell broke loose.

One of the officers smashed the main window and two flash bangs were thrown in. The one in front used the battering ram on the door, and the guy behind him tossed a flash bang in. One by one they charged in, yelling for the occupant to get on the floor.

For a moment he thought they had him.

With bated breath they waited for the sound of gunfire but there was none. A few minutes later the commander came out, shook his head, and gave a hand signal to indicate it was clear.

Ben moved in on the place with Dakota. He met the SWAT team coming out of the door.

"The place is empty."

Ben stepped inside and took in his surroundings. It was your typical hunter's cabin with a couch, one bedroom, a washroom, and a small kitchen. Everywhere they looked, animal skins could be seen on the walls and floors. The cabin itself was in a state of complete disarray. Dirty dishes filled up the sink, a smell of vegetables that had gone off lingered in the air. Ashtrays were overflowing with cigarette butts and god knows what else. He lifted one of them up and turned it and the butts were stuck to it. They began moving through the house looking for anything that might give them an indication of where he'd gone.

"Do you know if he has another place?"

"Ted might know. I'll go speak with him."

Ben wasn't used to seeing game wardens on site. But

that's how they handled it in Maine. They had their own specialty team that handled evidence recovery, forensic mapping, and special investigations along with the park rangers, who sometimes brought in ISB which was their own investigation service branch based out at the Atlantic Field Office.

"Ben, you might want to take a look at this," Nate called out to him from the basement. He made his way down into a dimly lit concrete hole in the ground that was damp. One light bulb lit up the unfinished basement. Mounted animal heads covered the walls like a blanket in a horror house. At the far end of the basement was a wooden desk. A light was turned on and a variety of small animals were laid out in preparation for taxidermy. The center of the basement was covered in a pool of blood. It was thick, crimson, and fresh. Attached to one of the steel beams was a pair of bloodied handcuffs.

"What do you make of that?"

Nate had touched some of it and brought it up to his nose to smell. "Pretty sure it's an animal."

A large white freezer was open. Inside were frozen chunks of meat but it wasn't the meat Nate wanted to show him. It was a metallic cocktail shaker. He'd already pried off the lid to show him what was inside. It was Chloe's purple cell phone. He recognized it because he had bought her the protective cover.

"That's how he sent the photo."

It also explained why they were unable to get a trace on her phone. It was a known fact in the counter-surveillance community that if you placed a cell phone in a steel cocktail shaker by itself, it would prevent eavesdropping through the microphone, block electric fields, and stop data from being transmitted. Refrigerators and freezers were meant to do the same but were not as effective as a stainless steel cocktail shaker.

"That photo had an image of a steel bed. It doesn't match the one that's inside this cabin, he must have been holding her somewhere else."

"Seems odd he would have kept it. Wouldn't you have got rid of it?"

"Souvenir? A means to taunt? Who knows?"

Nate nodded.

"See what prints you can pull off the phone."

Ben had to give his daughter props, the fact that she had grabbed her phone before being taken gave him some glimmer of hope. She was a smart kid. If anyone could get out of the situation, it was her. He glanced at the blood and hoped that it wasn't too late.

Right then Dakota returned with Ted Bishop in tow. He grimaced.

"Ugh. Some people are animals," he muttered as he edged his way around the mess. "You wanted to see me?" He looked at the cell phone that another officer was bagging.

"Are you aware of any other properties Mr. Adams owns in the Vassalboro area?"

Ted spread his hands. "Not that I know of, this was his home."

"No, I mean for hunting?"

He shook his head. "No clue."

Ben glanced at his hand. “What did you do to your hand?”

A white bandage was wrapped around his hand and went up underneath his coat.

“ATV mishap.”

“Lucky you didn’t hurt your other hand or your face,” he said, seeing how Ted’s other hand had no cuts or scratches.

“Yeah, guess I got lucky.”

“You’re his friend, right?” Ben asked.

“That’s right.”

“What can you tell me about him?”

His eyes widened, and he blew out his cheeks. He shifted from one foot to the next. “Not a lot to tell, really. He grew up in the area the same as me. He wanted to become a game warden but didn’t get through the hiring process. Keeps out of trouble.”

“Did he ever join the military?”

“No.”

“You?”

Ted hesitated before he replied. "Marine Corps."

"How long?"

"Two years."

"Enlistment is for four years minimum. What happened?"

"Does it matter?" He became defensive. "Not to be rude but what has this to do with finding Douglas?"

Ben paused and looked at him, studying his mannerisms. There was a lot you could pick up from people by the way they stood, the speed they spoke at, shifts in tone, and small gestures they made.

"Maybe I'm curious. I was in the military," Ben said.

"Then I shouldn't need to explain."

There were only a few reasons you didn't complete your enlistment contract. Medical, you went AWOL, or were dishonorably discharged.

"Anything else, Dr. Forrester?"

"No, that's it for now."

He watched him leave. Dakota was about to follow him out when Ben called her over.

"See what you can dig up on Adams having a place or renting one in Vassalboro, and I want an APB put out on Douglas Adams."

"I'm on it."

Chapter 35

Chloe knew the only way she was getting out of this was if she escaped. She'd seen his face, knew his name. Whatever sick, twisted fantasy he had about her, he was going to play it out without the other sicko.

It had been several hours since she had seen him. He'd received a phone call and had gone upstairs. His voice raised and then she heard him slam the door. The sound of a truck pulling away and the silence that followed meant she was alone. There was no way of telling when he would be back but this was her only chance if she could just get the handcuff off her leg.

It was cold down in the basement. It couldn't have been more than fifteen feet wide. The fact that he hadn't hidden her behind a wall or somewhere that was out of sight of the window made her think that they were in some isolated area. A place where people wouldn't hear her scream.

Her eyes scanned for anything she could use to escape. She sprawled out on the floor and reached for the table he had set up for taxidermy. If she could pull it towards her, she could tip it over and grab one of the taxidermy tools he'd been using. She'd seen him using sharp tools like wooden handled ice picks except thinner and angled slightly. One of them would work.

She pummeled the floor in frustration, tears streaking her cheeks as the tips of her fingers touched the table. Not wishing to be defeated she stood up. Her body ached. At least he hadn't drugged her.

The closest thing to her was a plank of wood leaning up against the wall. It was an awkward size that would have made it difficult to throw but if she could tip it onto the chair in front of the table, she might just be able to drag the wheeled chair back to her then use that.

Using all one hundred and twenty pounds of body weight she slammed into the wood, trying to knock it away from the wall. The handcuff bit into her ankle bone, causing her to scream in agony. *One more time, you can do this*, she told herself. The skin around her ankle was red and torn. She pushed again, throwing her entire body into it, using every ounce of effort to shift the piece of wood.

It wouldn't budge. Sweat rolled down her back as she huffed and panted. Please, God, if you get me out of here I will do anything. One more try, this time it barely moved a few inches. For a moment, she faced the possibility that perhaps she wouldn't be able to do this. The very thought was like gasoline to fire, it only motivated her more. She was going to shift that piece of wood if it meant breaking her bone in the process. Taking a few more steps back, she threw herself even harder at it. The last few times were agonizing.

One more hit and she would be done, the pain was too much. It wasn't the force of hitting the wood as much as it was the metal tearing into her ankle. It felt like someone had peeled back a blister and was rubbing salt into an open wound.

Enraged, she gave it one last attempt. *Move, you bloody*

piece of crap. She gave it one almighty heave and felt it shift. It wasn't the wood that was heavy but rather the amount of junk stuck behind it.

Panting, she wiped her brow with the back of her arm, feeling a glimmer of hope. Encouraged by the shift she gave it another giant push. It tipped and came crashing down on top of the wheeled chair, knocking it closer to her. She waited, listening intently and hoping that he hadn't returned. There was no sound. Quickly, she leaned forward and brought the chair back towards her. It was a small office chair on wheels. She lifted it to chest height and threw it as hard as she could at the tools on the table.

There was an almighty crash and clatter as indistinguishable metal tools, screwdrivers, needle-nosed pliers, a hand saw, and a wrench fell to the ground. Back down on her front she reached out for whatever was closest but they were still out of reach. She screamed in frustration. She was never going to get out of this hellish nightmare. Looking out the window she saw the sun beginning to wane behind the trees.

Chapter 36

Ben wasn't taking time off from the chase. Every waking hour was spent searching for answers. Outside the weather was getting bad. Inside lights kept flickering on and off. The rain beat against the windows, making it look like worms wiggling down. They had put out an APB on Douglas. Despite pressure from the town council and Chief Danvers, officers were handing out leaflets showing the faces of those missing. Chloe's was one of them. They had never done this before. It would have been an understatement to say that this hadn't caused a great deal of concern in the small town of Eden Falls with the locals and powers that be.

The island attracted millions of visitors every year. He had to wonder how this would affect the place in years to come. In the event they caught this sicko, and the town became known for the murders, would people still flock here in droves? Yes. That was the unfortunate part about any case. There would always be those with a morbid fascination with murder.

The table was laid out with photos of the women who had been found dead as well as those who had gone missing and were never seen again. Ben stared into the eyes of each of them, hoping to find a clue. Something, anything, he could latch onto.

There was a knock at the door. He laid his reading glasses down and went to see who it was. Dakota was glancing around when he opened the door. She was soaked from the rain.

"Ben."

He moved to one side. "Come on in."

Back inside she shook her hair and removed a long rain jacket. He asked her if she wanted a drink. "No, not while I'm working." She glanced at his glass as he poured himself another.

"I spoke with Jason Whittling today. You know, the one Jake Ashton said he was with on the night Chloe disappeared. Seems he was able to corroborate his alibi."

"And Earl?"

"He said he was asleep when he left that evening."

She ran her hand over the photos on the table and looked at him with concern.

"You can catch a few hours if you want."

He smiled at the offer. "I wish."

He had barely slept at all since she'd been taken. He knew the odds of finding her alive decreased with each passing day. Most were murdered within the first twenty-four hours. But there was something different about this killer.

"I think he's holding them. Collecting. I've looked over these women and some of them go back as far as six years. Now, the Patricia Welling girl was gone three years. The coroner said her neck was broken, but she died from drowning."

"So she couldn't get up."

He nodded. "Drowned in a few inches of water."

"What else?"

"I think he knew his victims."

"But didn't you say that these were all women from outside of the area?"

"Patricia wasn't. That got me looking these girls up online. Let me show you something."

Ben walked over to a desk, tapped the track pad on his notebook and the screen illuminated the last webpage he was on. It was for Eden Falls High School. The page was for the school yearbook and the date was for the class of 2012.

"Every single one of these girls but Chloe is from the same class, they all had markings on their bodies. They were all residents of Eden Falls or Tremont at one time. And look…"

He enlarged the image of a young male face. It was Douglas Adams.

"I'm telling you, we find him, we have our man. Any luck on that APB?"

She shook her head. "Not so far but state police and U.S. marshals are searching."

Ben leaned back in his chair and took a good sip of his

scotch.

"What is it?" he asked.

"Something doesn't add up. Why did he keep the cell phone? I mean, sure he was able to send the photo. Perhaps it was just for taunting or a memento, but it's risky, right? Besides, he doesn't strike me as someone familiar with counter-surveillance."

"You don't need to be. This stuff is out there on the net. Heck, people are learning how to make homemade bombs from manuals given away online."

Ben took hold of the photo of Patricia.

"He never strangled this one." He tapped his fingers against the side of his face. Outside the storm was getting worse.

"Maybe it was just part of changing his M.O.," she said.

"No," he leaned forward and tapped his finger on some of the other photos of dead women. "His crimes escalated. At first he was making it look like an accident, then, strangulation." He paused. "These kinds of killers don't dial back. They escalate."

"What do you mean?" she asked.

"With each murder the level of exhilaration gets less. It's like a drug. At first everything is new and exciting and the high is beyond anything they have experienced. Eventually they need more to maintain the same high. But it's not enough. They need something else to amp it up. Strangulation. Looking into their eyes as they die. It's one more step up the ladder. For some that's murder, for others it's rape, and another torture. They don't go back to what they used to do. It doesn't hold the appeal that it once had. He liked this one, otherwise he would have strangled her. He wanted her to be found this way. But why?"

Outside a crack of thunder erupted, startling both of them. "Tomorrow I want to swing by the high school and see if we can speak to one of the teachers."

Dakota nodded. "Well, I should get going."

"You can stay… if you want," Ben muttered.

She hesitated as though she was considering it.

"There's plenty of room right now. I'm just going to sleep out here."

"I don't know. Might get people talking."

"And that's a bad thing?"

"It can be in a town this small."

"I don't imagine many people are going to be stepping out tonight for an evening stroll, Woods."

"Are you sleeping in there?" She gestured to the sunroom.

"It's surprisingly comfortable."

It was close to nine at night.

"Thanks but, I prefer my own bed."

He shrugged. "Suit yourself."

She studied his face for a second before turning to get her coat. Ben looked her over. Sex was a great stress reliever. Maybe it was the drink prompting him but she was a good-looking woman. He shook the thought from his mind. "I'll let myself out. See you tomorrow bright and early."

"You bet," he replied.

Chapter 37

That night Ben's sleep was plagued again with nightmares of his wife and Adam. Bruns had torn him apart. Even now he still had his invisible hooks in him. Waking up, his body was soaked in sweat as he returned to his bed upstairs. He had to pass by Chloe's bedroom on the way. He wept at the thought of not being there for her. It was every father's worst nightmare.

It was only made worse by the phone call in the middle of the night.

When the phone rang, he glanced at it. He didn't recognize the numbers; it came up 000-000-0000. He was tempted to answer it. But if it was Bruns he really didn't need the head games. Jinx slept beside him on the bed. He watched the way she would dip her snout into Chloe's room, and whimper expecting to find her. She hadn't been the same since she was gone. Dogs had a sense of when something was not right.

And since she was gone, nothing had been right.

He couldn't imagine life without her now. While he remained strong for her through the loss of her mother and brother, what she didn't realize was that she was the only reason he got up each day and soldiered on. She brought life and light to his life, something that no amount of words could convey.

The rain continued battering the island through the night though weakening slightly as the sun began to rise. He'd managed to get four hours. Drinking to go to sleep worked but it also kept him awake. The alarm clock was flashing four in the morning when he went downstairs. He took his Glock 22 with him and Jinx slinked behind in his shadow.

He paused briefly at Chloe's door and glanced inside. His stomach sank again and his resolve to find her strengthened. He wouldn't shy away or break under the weight of what he was feeling. She needed him.

Downstairs he walked into the kitchen and put the kettle on. He splashed some cold water on his face to clear away the fog of sleep. He glanced at his calendar on the wall; he had forgotten his appointment with Emily Rose. He'd been making progress going twice a week to the therapy sessions but it hadn't stopped the dreams. She said they would continue for some time, then eventually fade. Subconsciously he wondered if he was clinging to them. Perhaps, he was scared of losing the memory of what Elizabeth looked like. Of course he had photos but it wasn't the same. It was as if he needed to see her dead to punish himself. It was as if the guilt of not finding her in time found its way to the surface when he slept because in the day he buried it below a blanket of self-loathing and drinking.

Ben filled a cup with boiling water and dropped a regular bag of Orange Pekoe into it. He'd never been one for the flavored teas. Elizabeth loved them. He called them hippie teas.

Shuffling over to the table he breathed in deeply and started flipping through the reports. He was sure that he was overlooking something, like a minor detail. To anyone else it would be inconsequential but it was the insignificant details that could crack a case.

University students were always asking him what it took to catch them. They only saw the ones he'd caught, never those that had slipped through his fingers or the ones that had fallen through the cracks of a faulty justice system.

The truth was you had to become obsessed and immerse yourself. You had to be willing to let it eat away at you in the middle of the night. You needed to think like them, go to the places in your mind that repulsed others. Only then, and with a good amount of luck could you hope to catch those who operated from a place of darkness.

Turning on his computer he brought up the yearbook again of the class of 2012. He scanned the faces. There were five areas labeled: *Photo not available.* No names were below them.

He looked at Douglas Adams.

What had made him do it? Had he taken her? Ben

thought back to the many criminals he'd interviewed in prison and the research he'd done in understanding the mind of a murderer.

There were always patterns in their lives. Something they had learned in their development that motivated their murders. No one in their thirties suddenly decided to one day become evil and commit an act of murder. The behavior had been developed long before that. It remained hidden below the surface, deep inside their childhood.

They weren't all from broken homes. Many had good families, stable and with two parents. Some had IQs that were high, above the normal range. But whether their home life looked stable on the surface, there was always something dysfunctional occurring below. A mental illness, emotional or sexual abuse was common. Those who killed usually had a cold relationship with their mothers. Often it was found that they were deprived of love.

Every single one of those that Ben had interviewed had

told him that they had experienced mental or physical abuse and yet this wasn't what they felt had damaged them. It was the sense of growing up feeling as though they weren't wanted. Neglected and left to their own devices they soon turned their attention to hurting animals. In many ways they were a product of a society that *hadn't* taught them to interact with compassion.

The lack of socialization and love formed their view of the world; a detached, cold, and unloving environment. Was it any wonder that they acted as they did?

Ben closed his computer and quieted his mind before the day began. It was five in the morning. He sipped his tea. Usually he treasured these moments but now all he could think about was Chloe.

Chapter 38

Less than two hours later, Ben and Dakota pulled up outside Eden Falls High School. It was a typical high school in desperate need of updating. It resembled a prison more than a school with its sun-bleached walls and metal-framed lower windows. Dakota told him they'd experienced enough vandalism that it warranted the update.

He tossed his coffee into the green garbage can outside, and headed in. The school had just broken for summer vacation. By now, Chloe would be off enjoying a full twelve weeks of downtime. Ben usually took her somewhere warm, anywhere that wasn't Florida. But she was older now, heading into her last year of high school. In previous years they had gone to Bermuda, and she'd taken a school buddy with her.

They entered the principal's office and were greeted by Linda Burton. She was a wiry woman in her late fifties.

Slightly on the larger size, causing her to walk on the edges of her feet.

"Morning," she said, shaking Ben's hand then Dakota's. "Come into my office."

Ben held a chair out for Dakota who found it amusing. It was a small room. Cabinets took up most of the space, a coffee maker was on a side table, and there was a large mahogany desk with a leather chair behind it. The blinds were closed, sealing out the bad weather they were still having.

"So how can I be of help?" Burton asked.

"You were the principal back in 2012?"

Her eyes opened wide. "That's right. Seems like only yesterday."

"How long have you been working here?" Dakota asked.

She leaned back in her chair and exhaled. "It's got to be nearly twenty-five years."

She seemed almost unsure. Though age had a way of fading memory.

"Do you recall Douglas Adams as a student?" Ben asked.

"Of course. How could I forget? Why, is he in trouble?"

"What can you tell us about him?"

She blew out her cheeks, trying to recall. "He was a challenging kid. So, it's good to see he became a ranger here in the park. I had my doubts about him I must say."

"Why?"

"Ah, it wasn't so much him as it was his parents. His mother. He tended to skip school a lot and when he did show up he showed signs of abuse. Never clothed too well. Almost neglected. He was given the bare essentials. We had her up here. What was her name?" She brought a finger to her lips. "Mary. That's right. Mary Adams. Strange woman. Very harsh sounding. She smoked a lot and from what I know she passed away of cancer about three years ago."

"Three?"

"Yeah, I could be wrong, though I'm pretty sure that's

what it was."

"And oh, what was he like when he was here? His studies and such?"

"A very bright lad, actually. Surprising, really. I remembered telling his mother that and finding her reaction troubling."

"In what way?"

She leaned forward. "Well, most mothers beam with delight if you say anything nice about their kid but not her. Oh no, she was very um… what's the word?"

"Cold?"

"Yeah. No sense of pride in him. I mean, how can anyone hope to stay on track if they are surrounded by apathy? Sad really. But it happens."

"What did his mother do?" Ben asked.

"Seamstress I believe."

"And the father?"

"He wasn't around. Walked out on them, she said."

Dakota nodded.

"What is this about?"

"We're just following up on a few enquiries."

"About the murders? Are you any closer to finding them?"

Ben twisted around and pulled out his tablet from a brown leather bag. He opened it and placed it on the table. "These girls. Did they ever complain about Douglas?"

"Not that I recall."

"And Douglas, did he ever interfere with any of the girls at the school?"

"He kept to himself. That's all I can tell you. I'm sure I could bring up his files and locate his test results but I don't think it's going to show you much."

"If you could do that, that would be appreciated," Dakota said.

"Oh by the way. Where did his mother live?"

She gave them the address. It wasn't the same as the one they had raided. While Dakota was getting a printout of his files, Ben checked his voicemail. There was one from Nate telling him that they hadn't found anything else at his home but they had managed to get a partial print off the phone. So far there hadn't been any sign of Douglas. It was just another kick in the gut.

Ben stood at the window looking out over the school playground. A tattered basketball net blew around in the wind and leaves rolled across the concrete like tumbleweeds. He was reminded of his years in high school and what his own family life was like. His father worked in security, his mother was a nurse. His fascination with criminals began long before he ever left school. He remembered it well. When he was ten, every morning following a night shift, his father would toss the newspaper on the table while he had breakfast. Ben would double-check the answers his father had scribbled in the crossword. On the opposite page, he remembered an article about a series of killings that occurred over a span of two years. Every month there was a new one. The perpetrator would break in, tie up his victims, rape them, and then decapitate them. Then using their blood, he had written the words, "Please catch me. I can't stop."

Now any rational person might think that he would simply turn himself in, but this wasn't a rational individual. It was hard to imagine that someone could do these grisly murders and then ask to be caught. Eventually he was cornered after one of the victims managed to escape while he slept beside her. He shot himself before the police got to him.

Those were the kind of people he'd dreamed of catching. Ben wanted them to spend their lives behind bars and eventually face the death penalty. He never knew until later the toll it would take on him or others. Some quit the FBI because of nightmares, others experienced peculiar medical conditions that disappeared once a case was over. Most just suffered from anxiety attacks. Catching criminals wasn't glamorous, it was soul destroying.

"You ready to go?" Dakota said, holding a folder with Douglas's information.

Ben nodded and thanked the principal.

Just before leaving he turned back. "Oh by the way, in

the Class of 2012, there were five spaces where there weren't any photos or names."

"Yeah, we tend to get some students who don't make it into the yearbook."

"Why?"

She seemed taken aback by the question. "Some chose inappropriate dress, others were absent, some didn't submit a photo, and others didn't wish to be included."

"Could you email me the names of those five?"

"Sure I can, though it will take a while to dig them out." She pulled out a piece of paper and a pen and Ben jotted down his email.

Chapter 39

The handcuff he'd placed around her ankle hurt but it was better than being tied to a bed. The other guy didn't want her getting away easily but this one seemed different.

Where was he? And why had he unlocked the door back at the last location? If he'd wanted her to escape why bring her here? None of it made sense.

She looked down at her restraint.

It wasn't impossible to get out of a pair of handcuffs; her father had shown her enough times. Heck, if she had a bobby pin or paperclip on her she would have been out of them by now. The trick was to wedge it into the keyhole, pivot and the ratchet mechanism that pushed up against the teeth would come loose. It was designed that way in the event that a key lock jammed or broke off inside. Police used a flexible handcuff shim just like a hairpin. It did the same thing.

She sat on the cold ground. It was quiet in the house, all she could hear was the sound of rain pounding outside. He hadn't returned in hours. She'd spent the entire night there alone, cold, uncomfortable, hungry, and thirsty. She'd relieved herself as far away from the post as she could stretch. But it was beginning to smell and stink up the place.

Every muscle in her body ached.

You're going to get out of here, she reminded herself. *You won't die like this.*

Had the other girls told themselves the same thing? She wanted her father, where was he?

Over the past two years she'd been hard on him. She knew he blamed himself for the death of her mother and brother. But it was out of his control. Still, she didn't know where to place the blame. She'd always seen him as her protector. He was an FBI agent for god's sake. That meant something to her. It meant they would be safe. But that wasn't true. He couldn't watch her every hour of the day.

She'd been resistant to her father wanting to move, then to his constant need for her to learn how to protect herself. *Like that had helped.* How do you protect yourself from a masked man who comes into your bedroom in the middle of the night? Who holds a knife to your throat and threatens to kill your grandmother if you don't go with him?

With her hands free, and one leg not restrained, it frustrated her knowing the tools on the table could get her out of the cuffs. The floorboard creaked above her. Her eyes flicked up. Every time she heard a sound, fear crept over her. The thought of him or the other one returning before she got out scared her like nothing else. Though, if it hadn't been for the ranger she would have been dead. But he was no better. She shook her head at the thought of it all. *A park ranger responsible for the disappearances!*

The basement was small but larger than the room she'd been held inside. It would be easier to escape here — if she could just get out. Right now though, it may as well have been solitary confinement.

The tools lay on the table teasing her. Chloe cast a glance at her ankle then around the room. She had to try again. Moving herself back across the floor, her feet felt numb from the cold. She reached the chair with outstretched fingers and yanked it back.

Closing her eyes, saying a silent prayer, she flung the chair again.

When it didn't work, she tried again.

Quit.

Chloe heard the word inside her head. But she wasn't going to give them the satisfaction. Even if it killed her, she was going to fight to get out of here.

Tired. Stiff and feeling so much pain in her ankle, she stared bleakly at the chair. It was impossible to get out. But what other choice was there?

Helpless but not quitting, Chloe crawled back over to the chair, feeling the teeth of the handcuff bite her skin once again.

Chapter 40

They were minutes from arriving at Douglas's mother's old residence when Ben's cell phone vibrated and skipped around in the middle console. He swerved to the hard shoulder and took a look to see who was calling. It was Nate. He jabbed answer.

"Ben, we have him."

"What?"

"Douglas Adams, he just walked into the station ten minutes ago."

He frowned. "Are you kidding me?"

"No, I'm looking at him right now."

"Was anyone with him?"

"No."

"Who's with him now?"

"Danvers."

"I'll be there in five."

Ben hung up and swerved away from the side of the

road at breakneck speed. He slammed his foot to the metal as he gunned it around the loop road heading for Eden Falls Police Station. Rain was falling heavily by now. The sky had opened up, pounding the roof of the car and making the roads slippery and dangerous. As they exploded past a clearing that overlooked the ocean, a thick mist had rolled in reducing visibility. Even the white lighthouse in the distance couldn't be seen.

* * *

Once they arrived at the station, Ben approached Nate. He was standing behind a two-way mirror scrutinizing Douglas and taking in every word.

"Oh hey," he motioned to the interview room.

"What's he said?" Ben asked.

"Not much really. He said he was out of town visiting a guy by the name of Wes Rayland, a friend of his who works as a ranger over in Bangor."

"What park?"

"Baxter State Park. Danvers has already made the call and confirmed the alibi."

Ben placed a hand on his hip and ran the other over his head.

"I want in."

Nate nodded and led the way. When the door opened Chief Danvers was coming out.

"Not much there. But we have enough to hold him overnight," Danvers said.

"Hold overnight? We have my daughter's cell phone found at his cabin."

"We've taken prints but until we have a match or your daughter shows up, it's all circumstantial right now, Ben. I'm sorry."

Dakota walked into the room. Ben took off his suit jacket, never once taking his eyes off Douglas who was looking down. For a moment Ben just stared at him, observing his body movement, his mannerisms. The way he picked at his nails and sniffed as though he was going to walk.

"How did you come to have my daughter's cell phone at your cabin?"

He glanced up. His eyes darted nervously between Ben and Dakota.

"Someone must have placed it there. I didn't take it. I certainly didn't take your daughter."

"And the flask it was found in?" Ben didn't say it was a cocktail shaker on purpose.

He shrugged. "I'm as confused as you are. Like I told Danvers I went out of town to see a friend."

"Why?"

"We went through training at the same time. I hadn't caught up with him in a while."

"But why now when this investigation is going on?"

"I'm not an investigator. Just a park ranger."

Ben paced around the room slowly.

"Why did you turn yourself in?"

He shrugged and raised his hands. "Someone told me the police were looking for me."

"Who?"

"Ted Bishop."

"So you have no idea of how that cell phone ended up

in your cabin."

"Nope."

"Is there anyone else who uses your cabin?"

"Yeah, Ted. Any animals that we bring back from hunting we skin there."

"You mentioned you did some hunting in Vassalboro. That's two hours away. You don't skin them there?"

"No. As you probably could tell from the basement. It creates quite a mess."

"Why do it inside?"

"Why not?"

"Give me the address of the place in Vassalboro."

He shook his head. "I don't know it."

"You hunt there but you don't know the address?"

"It's in the middle of privately owned farmland. Ted drives."

Ben placed his hands on the table, inhaled deeply, and leaned in.

"What is the address?"

"I told you I don't know."

"Of course." He blew his cheeks out, straightened up, and in a matter of seconds shot around the table, grabbed hold of Douglas, threw him up against the wall, and was shaking him as Dakota tried to get him off.

"Listen up, you dumb fuck. You're gonna give me that address."

"I don't know it," he yelled as Nate burst into the room along with Danvers. "Ted does."

"Ben, let him go. Ben!" Nate shouted at him and Danvers struggled to pull him back. He was breathing hard and staring intently into Douglas's eyes. Danvers still had hold of him. Ben shooed him off.

"Alright. Alright."

"Get him out of here," Danvers hollered.

"You aren't prepared to do what is necessary."

"Out," Danvers yelled.

"Don't worry, I'm gone."

Ben grabbed his jacket off the back of the chair and left the room. Dakota was on his heels. Outside he went and got some water. He swallowed hard and tossed the triangle paper cup at the trash.

"You gonna be okay?" Dakota asked.

Ben looked at her then at Nate.

"When I asked Ted if he knew about a property in Vassalboro, he told me he didn't. Now one of them is lying and my money is on this freak."

Nate ran a hand around the back of his head.

"Why don't you go home, Ben? I'll call you if there's been any development."

Ben scowled. "Would you, Nate? If it was your kid…"

Nate looked over at his shoulder and let out an exasperated sigh. The lights flickered, went off and then power came back on again.

"Look, the weather's getting worse, there's not much more we can do today."

Ben began heading for the door.

"Where are you going?"

"His mother's house."

"I'm coming with you," Dakota said.

* * *

Outside the rain was battering the ground, making every step treacherous. Ben and Dakota made a dash for the car. The rain plastered their hair against their foreheads and drenched their clothes in a matter of seconds.

Inside, Dakota shook her head. Ben turned over the ignition and let the windshield wipers do their job. It was blowing sideways so hard they could barely see a few feet in front of them.

"It doesn't look as if it's going to let up any time soon."

Ben smashed his fist against the steering wheel, unleashing pent-up frustration, then looked up through the torrential downpour.

"Just give me one break. For god's sake. That's all I'm asking for."

Chapter 41

Douglas Adams's mother's home looked derelict, abandoned, a real dump. Buried deep in two acres of pine forest, a long, winding dirt driveway led up to a round clearing. It was eight miles from Eden Falls Harbor. With the wind tearing through the forest and rain turning soil into a muddy slip and slide, Dakota and Ben shielded their faces. She had tried several times to reach Ted Bishop by phone to discuss the matter of the Vassalboro address but he wasn't answering.

Ben swept the area with his flashlight.

"You know we need a search warrant," Dakota said.

"Screw that."

She wasn't going to argue with him. Emotions were riding high and he'd already overstepped his boundaries. A few more wouldn't make much difference. When they climbed the steps that led up to the front entrance, Dakota's foot went through the weathered wooden steps.

Ben spun around. "You okay?"

"Just dandy." She caught the railing just in time but her leg was grazed.

The place hadn't been updated in years.

With Dakota hobbling behind him, they circled around until they got to the main door. Ben stood back and kicked it just off to the left of the lock. It didn't move. One more and the frame groaned from the impact.

"I must have found the only piece of solid wood on the property," he said right before he kicked it again. This time it burst open, wooden shrapnel exploded in every direction and the door hung awkwardly.

Both of their flashlights illuminated the inside of the dusty cabin. Dakota flipped the light switch up and down but nothing came on. It was hard to tell if the place had power or if the storm had knocked it out. They had to rely on the glow of their flashlights in order to see anything. All the furniture inside was covered in white sheets making it feel even more eerie than without.

A flash of sheet lightning, a few seconds of seeing

clearly, then they were enveloped in darkness again. It was musty inside like a home that hadn't been aired out in weeks. The entire place was made from cedar wood. It was commonly used on the island.

"It doesn't even look lived in," Ben said.

"Maybe he couldn't bring himself to sell the property."

"By the sound of the way she treated him you would think he would have demolished it."

Dakota picked up a photo frame and blew off the dust. It was an image of a young Douglas with his mother. She looked strict. It was unlike most family photos where a parent would be hugging their child or smiling. They stood stoic in front of the camera, no contact between them.

She placed it down and moved her way around the furniture into the bedroom area. Everything was draped in cloth. She ran her fingers across the top of the sheet, picking up a thin layer of dust. These hadn't been moved in months, maybe years. She coughed breathing in some of it. Ben was next door rooting through drawers.

She shone the light inside the closet, up into the corners. She ran her hand up around the top ledge but there was nothing except dust. On the rack above the clothes was a wicker box, to the side of that a brown towel and on the racks floral dresses. As she crouched down, her eyes drifted over three pairs of flat, sensible-looking shoes. The kind that were worn by women who weren't looking to attract attention. She shifted them to the side to get a better look at something in the corner. It didn't take her long to realize what it was when it shot out and scared her half to death.

It was a mouse. She let out a squeal and Ben came into the room and spotted the critter before it vanished into the woodwork. He chuckled.

"Glad you find it amusing. Find anything?"

"No, just a lot of junk, and large crucifixes."

He went back out, and she pulled down the box. Inside was an old pocket watch. She flipped it open. The hands had stopped. Besides that, it contained a small purse of old coins and a Bible. She took it out and rubbed her hand over the leather exterior. It was an old King James.

She flipped it open and thumbed through the crinkled yellow paper. Small notes had been made in the margins in red. In the front was a handwritten note.

To Douglas,

Do what the Lord requires.

Mother.

Dakota's mind drifted back to her childhood. She'd grown up in a religious family. They weren't strict as much as they were hypocrites. Wearing one face on Sunday and another the rest of the week. Her mother drank hard and at times locked her in a room. Other times she was a sweet as pie. It was very Jekyll and Hyde. Her father was a minister, and her mother worked for a pregnancy crisis center. On the surface their lives were very idyllic. A good home, private schooling, and attending church every Sunday. But that was what the world saw. Behind the curtains, when all the crowds were gone, they were very different people. The need to preserve the façade of normality strained their marriage and by the time she was eleven her parents divorced.

Her mother took her and her younger sister and moved away. That's when the drinking really kicked in.

Dakota snapped back to the present when her phone began buzzing in her pocket. She took it out. The faint blue screen lit up her face. It was Danvers. Ben continued looking around as she took the call.

"Where are you?" he sounded as if he was on the move.

"At Mrs. Adams's residence."

He exhaled hard. "What the hell are you doing there?"

"What do you think?"

There was a beat. "Oh my god, does this guy do anything by the book?" Danvers asked.

She walked back into the living area. Outside the wind howled, pushing branches against the window like gnarled fingers raking back and forth. She pulled at a sheet to reveal an old piano beneath. The key tops were worn and some missing entirely. She pressed down on one and it let out an out-of-tune clang that echoed.

“What do you need?” she asked.

Dakota could hear the sound of sirens and Danvers barking orders to the officer driving.

“We’ve got a ten thirty-three from an officer in need of assistance in the vicinity of Blackwoods Campground.” She heard the sound of a door slam. “A possible abduction. This could be our man.”

That was the police code for a chase in progress.

“We’re five minutes away.”

She hung up. Ben was coming up from the basement shaking his head.

“Possible abduction,” she said, thumbing over her shoulder. “We need to go.”

She didn’t need to convince him, he was out the door before she was. The wheels on the car squealed and mud splashed up the sides as they tore out of there.

Outside the wind was causing all manner of

destruction. The weather had knocked down a power line. Wires hung awkwardly over the driveway, glowing orange sparks spat furiously from the top of a wooden post into the night.

"Did you find anything?"

"Nothing of use," Ben replied despondently.

Chapter 42

Dakota's dark blue Ford Crown Victoria burst into Blackwoods Campground almost losing control. Four cruisers flashing red and blue were already on scene. Two female officers were tending to a girl beneath a water-soaked porch. Beside them were three other women huddled together. It was chaotic from the moment they pushed out of the car.

Shouting, pointing, and complete noise from a vehicle with its siren still on.

Here we go. The snap of gunfire could be heard in the woods. There was no time to ask who was involved or what had happened. Both of them took off racing in the direction of where it was coming from, along with another officer.

The forest in the daytime was treacherous enough; one wrong footing and you could twist, or break an ankle. Now here they were sprinting beneath towering pines, down steep slopes, and over huge boulders. The only visibility came from flashlights and a crescent moon partially hidden behind dark clouds. The river and streams seemed louder than usual. With the amount of rain they'd had, it had caused the rivers to rise and turn the soil around into a landslide death trap.

"You see anything?" Dakota hollered.

Rain spilled off the top of Ben's forehead into his eyes as he squinted. It was useless. It was pitch-black. Occasionally flashlight beams cut the darkness then they'd disappear behind the black trees and mounds of underbrush. That's what made this place prime pickings for a madman. They could snatch a girl from a tent, or outside toilets, and disappear into the night without worry of being pursued. Hell, if Douglas had been responsible for taking the women, no one would have thought twice about being led away by a park ranger. But he was locked up, so who the hell had attempted to take another woman?

"Over here," an officer shouted. Then another one

yelled. It was all beginning to blur into one voice. Dakota headed in one direction while Ben went in the opposite. A bullet snapped and hit a tree close to Ben, his blood pressure shot up as he took cover behind a thick pine tree. His training had taught him not to start shooting wildly into the night. He had no way of knowing if it was an officer. This was exactly how friendly fire happened.

Satisfied that no more shots were being fired and driven by urgency, he continued running through the middle of the forest towards the sound of officers' radios and shouting. They must have been pursuing him for ten minutes. A chopper was in the air over the forest. Its large beam of light swept ahead of him. When he crested a section and looked down at where flashlights were flickering, he could see officers converging in on a secluded cabin tucked deep in the forest.

Then he noticed two figures running towards the main entrance.

Ben could hear officers yelling and telling someone to put the gun down. Desperate to get close he lost his footing, pitched forward, and rolled down the embankment. He reached out frantically looking for some way to stop himself from colliding with a tree. There was nothing except moss, and granite stone. As he picked up speed, dirt found its way up his pant legs, in his mouth, and all over his face. Finally, as he searched for a way to slow his descent, he latched on to a tree root. Catching hold, he nearly tore his arm out of the socket.

Covered in wet earth he coughed, spitting a chunk of it out. Unhurt but battered and bruised, he scrambled to his feet and pushed on, cursing the forest under his breath.

He tried to brush off the grime and compose himself as he hustled over to the cabin and was met by a sight that made his heart sink. Dakota had been shot. She was still alive but in need of a medic. An officer told him he'd already called for EMS. Ben dropped down and gripped her hand.

"Don't you go dying on me, Woods, remember, you still owe me a beer."

She coughed and smirked slightly at the sight that was before her.

"You look like shit," she said, groaning.

"Yeah, I think I might have swallowed some."

That only made her groan more.

The bullet had torn through her left shoulder. It didn't look critical but they would need to stop the bleeding. One of the officers was applying pressure as more gunfire erupted. This time it came from inside the house.

"I'll be back." Ben charged towards the house with his eyes on the front of his gun sight. Equal height, equal light, he muttered instinctively. He'd done it ever since he learned to fire a gun. It just became part of readying himself, just the way he checked if it was loaded. It referred to shooting in exact alignment. Making the front sight even with the top of the rear sight had become second nature — something he didn't even think about, but it always went through his head each time he pulled his piece.

Following behind an officer, he entered the cabin and

was met by the sight of Ted Bishop's lifeless body. Off to one side was a sick and twisted mask that was white and molded to look like an old man. A trap door was open and an amber light came up from it.

The officer pointed. "The chief and two other officers are already down there."

Ben didn't waste a second, he moved past the body, glancing at his bandaged arm. He carefully made his way down the wooden ladder. The hole was wide enough for one person. It went down about thirty feet before he landed on rocky ground. The smell of human flesh, mold, and stone permeated the air. Small lights hung every few feet. Loose stone crunched beneath his boots as he made his way along the makeshift tunnel. The sides and top were covered in wooden planks bolted into the stone to support it from caving in. Ben placed a handkerchief to his mouth and nose as he entered a space where the ceilings were higher. It didn't look as if it had been made by tools. Some areas were smooth as though they had been naturally formed. Much of the landscape on Mount

Desert Island was a combination of mud, sand, and volcanic rock.

The first room he saw off to his left was full of taxidermy products, tools, and two of the same masks that matched the one Ted had been wearing. He didn't linger there, his eyes were set on the rooms. *Chloe?* He moved down through them. Two officers had already opened the doors. He rushed along, desperately hoping that the next would hold Chloe. But none of them had women in them. They were empty. Only a single bed with a small table in each one.

"Sorry, Ben, she's not here, but Helen Hayes is still alive, an officer is bringing her out now," Chief Danvers said, sympathetically placing his hand on his shoulder before following out one of the officers. Ben breathed out hard, dropped down into a crouched position, and felt himself beginning to well up with tears. He ran both hands over his face and blew out hard.

What had they done? They'd shot the only one who could tell them where she was, if she had been here at all.

"Dr. Forrester, you might want to see this," an officer said, motioning towards the room he'd passed. He got up and followed him through another door that was smaller, off to one side. A light was already turned on, giving him a clear view of the grisly display.

"Oh my god."

His eyes surveyed all the women who had been murdered and subjected to taxidermy. Like a room full of mannequins, each of them had been posed and even dressed in skirts. Most had makeup applied to their lips and faces. Some were bent and twisted into sexual positions with all manner of lewd instruments attached. At the far back against the wall were others who'd had been mutilated in ways that made him grimace.

Ben diverted his eyes away. He brought a hand up to his mouth, thinking he was about to vomit. It was horrific. The sight made only worse, by having to walk by each one and examine them to see if his daughter was among them.

Though he was relieved at not finding Chloe, it didn't

decrease the anxiety. He could hear blood thumping hard in his ears as the world around him hung heavy on his chest. A migraine starting to come on fast. He reached into his pocket, pills clattered as he pulled out the medication. Twisting the cap, he tapped out two and tossed them back without water.

Perhaps he'd buried her? The thought of her being buried alive brought back the terror of the past.

Chapter 43

Tired, cold, thirsty and hungry. She couldn't bear it any longer.

Either he was going to kill her or leave her here to starve to death. The hours seemed to pass painfully slowly. No sense of time except the waning of light from the window. In the silence Chloe attempted to cling to what remained of her sanity. Her father's face and voice the only constant in her mind, as her inner strength began to fade away. She wasn't foolish. The odds were stacked against her. Exhaustion, low temperatures, and the need for something to drink and eat had become almost unbearable.

She knew it was bad when she saw a cockroach crawl across the floor. The thought of snagging it and eating it crossed her mind. Or when rainwater dripped from the window to the floor — her own personal Chinese water torture.

Or was it all just a hallucination? What had he injected in her? Her mind was beginning to unravel and play tricks on her. Had he left? Was he waiting for her to escape her binds only to toss her back down?

I'm going out of my mind…

Every attempt at getting close to the tools had failed. The only thing that kept her from quitting was the fear that she would die alone.

She had never been one to quit anything. Her father had drilled that into her from an early age. Change course, make another decision, but don't stop pushing forward, he would say.

Her mother had been the same. The few times she had fallen asleep she'd seen her mother. Had it been a dream or was she bordering on death?

Shivering, and aching with pain, she went back to repeating the same actions. It had to be a numbers game. Surely the odds would soon swing in her favor? The sudden clatter of the chair hitting the table and bouncing back, without any tools dropping, soon answered that.

Again. Do it again. It was no longer her voice she heard; it was her mother's. This time she bounced that thing sideways against the wall. Every time she held her breath, hoping this would be it.

"Screw you," she said loudly, shifting her frustration to the image of her captor in her head as she hurled that chair across the room. What was that? The twelfth, thirteenth, or fifteenth time she had tried? She had lost count.

Help me, Mom, she whispered under her breath

That was all she could do now. Pray to God and speak to her mother as though she was there with her. For so long she had blocked out the memory of her mother as a means of coping with the loss. Tears now streamed her cheeks. Her eyes welled up. All the frustration and pain of the loss came bubbling to the surface. In that moment her walls broke apart, and she wept hard as she continued to try and escape. Large chunks of drywall lay scattered all over the floor. Dust filled the air. Even a paint can was turned on its side, leaking out green goo.

Every new attempt brought with it a sense of hope then despair.

If it weren't for her mother and father's voice, she would have given up long ago.

Then it happened. She saw it. It clattered on the floor. For a second she didn't believe it.

Scrambling across the ground, she reached out, unable to grasp what could release her from this hell. Grappling the chair again she turned it on its side, held on to the backrest, and used the chair to extend her reach. Slowly, inch by inch, the steely sharpened tool got closer.

Chapter 44

This was going to be a long night in Eden Falls. The discovery of the missing would attract nationwide attention. Unlike the Bruns case where he got away, the police would be praised for acts of bravery and a job well done on this one. All the mistakes they had made prior to the capture would be swept under the carpet. The commissioner from the department of public safety and public relations people would spin this in the right direction. The FBI would move on to the next case with little more than a pat on the back while the local boys in blue would be placed on a pedestal. It was a short-lived game but the media would eat it up and milk it for all it was worth.

In less than an hour the place was cordoned off with police tape and swarming with the Bangor FBI agents, Nate, and EMS. Ben went out to speak with the Hayes girl that had been brought up. She had been placed on a stretcher by EMS and they were about to lug her out of the forest when he approached.

"Just a minute, I want a word."

They laid her back down. The girl was in shock. Her eyes wide and wild. She was your typical university girl, twenty-two and very attractive. The thought that she might have seen Chloe or heard her was the only hope he could cling to now.

Even though she was safe now, there was a palpable fear in her gaze. It would take years to work through the trauma she'd endured. Every victim was different. Some would appear as if they had bounced back with a new lease on life, giving talks around the country, while others would crawl into a shell of an existence.

"Helen, I'm Special Agent Benjamin Forrester of the FBI, I just had a few questions for you."

"Is Rachael dead?" she asked.

Ben hesitated for a second then nodded slowly. "I'm afraid so."

Tears welled up in her eyes.

"Did you get that bastard?" she spat.

"We did."

"What about the others?" Helen asked.

Her acknowledgement of a second suspect only confirmed his thoughts about Douglas's involvement. Hopefully they could bring her in and she could verify by sight or through hearing his voice.

"He's in custody. Helen, I need to know. My daughter was taken." Ben reached into his pocket and removed his wallet. He pulled out a crinkled photograph of Chloe and held it out so she could see.

"Did you see her or hear her at any point?"

She studied it hard then shook her head from side to side. Ben's heart sank. Presumably there were only two people who knew where she was. One of them was dead, and the other was in custody. He rose to his feet and watched two EMS guys carry her out. Dakota was being treated a short distance away.

Nate Mueller was talking with an officer before he came over and placed a hand on Ben's shoulder. "I'm sorry, man. Is there anything I can do?"

Ben's eyes dropped. "You think you can take a few guys over to Ted Bishop's home? Dakota will give you the address."

"You think he's keeping her there?"

"No idea. But I do know Douglas said Ted knew the address of the place they used to hunt at in Vassalboro. See if you can find an address at his place."

"What are you going to do?"

"Pay Douglas Adams another visit."

Nate squeezed Ben's shoulder before calling over a couple officers. Ben's eyes drifted over the scene. It would take them days to compile and photograph everything. Forensic specialists would dust for fingerprints and latent evidence. As the investigation expanded, no doubt the body count would climb. Bodies would be removed and taken to a forensic department for identification. It was going to blow this community apart, never mind those considering camping in national parks in other states.

Chapter 45

In a deserted cabin, nestled two hours away in Vassalboro just across the Kennebec River from Maine's capital, Chloe twisted the sharp tool furiously in the keyhole of the handcuffs. It was far more difficult than she'd anticipated. It wasn't that unlocking the cuffs was hard in itself as it was the tool that had fallen to the floor wasn't the right type. It was too wide. She needed something thinner, something that would bend but remain firm. There were two ways that she knew to unlock handcuffs without the key. One was inserting a thin pin and pushing the ratchet away from the teeth, the other was forcing a flat piece of metal in between the teeth while turning your wrist or ankle. Both relied on using the right tool. Everything she needed was either on the table or scattered out of reach on the floor below it.

Stay calm, she told herself. *Figure this out.*

It was hard to stay calm when, at any moment,

Douglas or the other man could return. By the time they showed up she needed to be as far away as possible.

What can I use?

That's when her eyes fell on the can of pop that she'd thrown at him. She grabbed a hold of the chair and once again began to use it to extend her reach. If she could just get it, she could empty out the pop, tear open the can, and use a piece of the metal.

She was in the process of trying to get it, frustrated that the can kept rolling, when she heard a sound outside. At first it was subtle then louder, like a large canister had been knocked over. Fearful that he'd returned, she propped the chair back up again and huddled against the wall. As she cowered like a scared animal waiting to be executed, her eyes swept the windows.

Maybe this was all part of his sick game; make her think he was gone and then reappear just as she got out. She listened intently trying to make out what it was.

The noise outside was a shuffle. It didn't sound like footsteps but she wasn't going to take any chances. Was it him or an animal? Perhaps a deer or a coyote? The thought of screaming had crossed her mind but if it was him she didn't want to give him any more reason to hurt her.

Please let it not be him... Oh god not now...

The sound became faint as if whatever or whoever had moved on.

She had no idea where he'd taken her but if she could get out and reach a phone, she could call her father. That was all that was pushing through her mind. *Stay calm. Get out. Escape.*

Still restrained, she felt a small amount of relief as silence fell over the place again. Her pulse raced as she returned to the task of trying to reach the can of pop. This time she moved faster.

Chapter 46

When Ben stepped into the cellblock at the county police department, he found more than he expected — Douglas Adams was hanging by a belt from the jail door.

"No, no!" he screamed, motioning to an officer. "Open this cell."

An officer hurried forward, turned over the lock, and slid back the steel door. Ben rushed in and hoisted him up by grabbing him in an NFL tackle right below his groin. The officer undid the leather belt from its place around the bar and Adams flopped down. Immediately he checked vitals. There was no pulse. He was stone cold.

Ben paced back and forth, running his hands around his neck and over his head trying to get a grip. It only took a few breathless seconds to realize that someone hadn't removed his shoes or belt.

"How the hell did he end up in here with this?"

It was normal procedure for anyone placed in a

holding cell to have their belt, shoes, socks, and the contents of their pockets removed. Additionally, all cells were monitored by closed-circuit TV as well as being checked physically. Douglas Adams still had all of his belongings on him.

The young officer shrugged.

He turned. "I'll ask one of the others."

"Hold on, where is the video stream?"

"Um, yeah… upstairs," he replied.

This was beyond a royal screw-up. Something was seriously wrong. Both of the men were now dead. Any chance of finding out where Chloe was or what had happened to her was gone.

Upstairs there were two officers manning the phones and front desk. Everyone else had been pulled out to the crime scene. He asked them the same question and both of them had no idea. A look of shock crossed their faces. Then they looked at each other as if they were about to shift the blame or hope the other would provide an answer, but there wasn't one. They were so short-staffed and overwhelmed by the influx of phone calls from locals wanting to know what was going on in the town, they hadn't paid any attention to monitoring the cellblock.

Ben followed the officer down to where they housed the recording equipment. Less than two minutes later they pulled up a streaming feed. *What the heck?* All it had recorded was from the time Douglas arrived at the station, to thirty minutes after, and then it was blank.

"How can that happen?"

He shrugged. "It's the storm. The power has been up and down all night."

"You don't have a backup generator?"

"Yes, of course we do, but it mustn't have kicked in."

He shook his head, trying to process the turn of events. Again they tried forwarding the stream but there was nothing but white noise.

Ben thought fast. He didn't want to believe it. What would be the point? He pulled his phone from his pocket and contacted Nate.

"Douglas Adams is dead."

“What?” Nate stammered.

“I don’t have time to explain.”

Nate cleared his throat. “Ben, hold on a minute. He’s dead?”

“Hung himself in the cell. Now, tell me you have found something.”

“Not much. Um. We’re still checking.”

Behind him he could hear officers rooting through belongings.

“Have you checked his truck?”

“Not yet.”

In the background he heard an officer mutter something. “Hold on a sec, Ben.”

Nate must have muffled the receiver with his hand. He could hear mumbles in the background.

“Ben. I’m holding a photograph of a hunting trip. Ted and Douglas are in it but so is Kurt Danvers.”

Chapter 47

A cold shiver shot through Ben. His mind churned over fast, filtering through all the reports, photos, crime scenes, and interactions he'd had since the start of the case. Why wasn't Douglas at his home when they raided it? The chief said he'd phoned through to find out if he was at work. Who was it that confirmed Douglas's alibi of being in Bangor? Danvers. Who could have placed him in the cell without removing his belt? Danvers. Then his thoughts went to what the Hayes girl had said. *Did you get the others?* Others? If there were only two she would have said, the other. Finally, his thoughts flipped to the room below the cabin, he'd seen two masks, but there was one upstairs beside Ted Bishop.

Ben twisted around. "Where's the chief?"

The officer looked flustered for a few seconds. "Um. He left here a while ago."

"How long?"

"Oh, Maybe an hour."

"The officer that called in the abduction attempt. Get him on the radio." The officer nodded and left the room. Ben got back on the phone with Nate. "I need you to get over to Chief Danvers's residence."

"Where's he live?"

Ben held the phone to his chest and called out to an officer but no one answered.

"I'll get back to you."

"Stay on the line, Ben," Nate said before barking orders to the officers who were still turning over objects in the house. Ben was on the move now. There was no time to waste. Back upstairs he asked an officer if she knew where Danvers lived. She said it was a beach house somewhere down by the water in Eden Falls. Beyond that they didn't know. Ben had them direct him to his office. He began rooting through papers on his desk, looking for anything that might show his local address. He tore out the drawers and had an officer going through a filing cabinet. One of the desk drawers was locked.

"You got a key for this?"

"No."

"You might want to back up." The officer did one better and double-timed it out of the room. Ben stepped to the side, pulled his Glock 22, and fired three rounds at the drawer. Pieces of wood shot out as he yanked hard on the handle and it came away. Inside it was full of papers. He began tossing them and frantically scanning each one. He'd made it through about eight pages when he came across several pieces of open mail. One was a utility bill. The address in the top left-hand corner was for a property in Vassalboro.

Nate was still on the line. "You there?"

"Yeah, go ahead."

It was a two-hour journey by car to Vassalboro.

"We're gonna need a police helicopter."

Chapter 48

She was bleeding but free of her restraint.

After countless miserable attempts to get the pop can, she finally managed to hook and roll it in her direction. Upon emptying the contents, tearing it open along with cutting her hand, she was able to use a piece of the metal to create her own makeshift handcuff shim. She'd inserted it into the same entrance as the ridged bar. By interrupting the ridged bar from engaging with the inner handcuff and by twisting her ankle outward, she was able to free herself.

Go! Get the hell out of here. It was the only plan that Chloe had left. She didn't even think to grab a tool as a weapon, instead she limped up the steep wooden staircase to the top. She twisted the doorknob only to find it was locked.

"No! No, no!" she screamed. Moving quickly, she went back down and searched around for the hammer she'd seen him using earlier. Tools and animal carcasses were scattered all over the ground. Scrambling around, she found it. She staggered back up the stairs with a new sense of purpose and determination and began beating the panels. After being held captive for all this time she wasn't going to let a piece of wood stand in her way.

It didn't take long to plow a hole big enough for her hand to get through. Splinters stuck into her arm as she reached through and unlocked it from the outside. A twist of the knob and she was out.

She hadn't stopped for a second to think if he was on the other side. Her heart was thumping in her chest. Tears streaked her face as the strain of captivity rushed to the surface.

Standing in a short hallway she turned to her left and right unsure of which way to go. The phone? Thirsty, she limped her way into a kitchen area. A flood of daylight from a large window burned her eyes. It was a cabin but where was it? All she could see were trees, bushes, and undergrowth outside. She twisted the tap, water rushed out and she ducked her face underneath and sucked in water until she was no longer thirsty. As she realized that she might be alone, her eyes swept the room for a phone. She moved into the small living area still gripping the hammer. She wasn't entirely convinced that he wasn't hiding and waiting to pounce.

There were no phones, no lines, not even a TV. Just the basics, a couch, chair, table, and fireplace. No photos hung on the walls. A staircase led up to a second floor. Maybe there would be one there. Without knowing where she was, she wasn't going to just flee immediately.

Upstairs she checked the rooms. Nothing.

She crawled forward across the landing, ready to head down when she heard the sound of spitting gravel. She froze. A sudden wall of fear hit her. In a flash she rushed to the window, panicking only to breathe a sigh of relief.

It was a police car from Eden Falls. *Dad?*

Instinctively she banged on the window but it pulled up around the side of the house. She couldn't have made it down the stairs any faster. The desire to get away from the house and her captor was so strong that she forgot the pain in her ankle. Still clasping the hammer, she scanned the front door, then the windows for the police.

Then something dawned on her.

Why was there only one police car? If they had figured out where she was, wouldn't there have been more? A SWAT team? EMS? Hell, the FBI!

One cruiser?

Petrified and confused she froze in place at the foot of the stairs.

Her hand tightened around the hammer upon seeing a large figure through the opaque glass door. A key went in. The doorknob turned.

Chapter 49

The private property in Vassalboro was so isolated and shrouded in woodland that it was virtually impossible to land close. Ben had notified state and local police in the Vassalboro region within minutes of being up in the air. Some of the officers in Eden Falls located the chief's residence in town and had already burst inside. Chloe wasn't there which only led him to believe that she'd been relocated.

The police officer who had called in for assistance when pursuing Ted Bishop had confirmed over the radio that Chief Danvers had instructed a dispatcher to get an officer over to Blackwoods Campground after a concerned camper had reported a prowler.

There was no record of any phone call being placed from Blackwoods.

Nate was already gathering phone records to determine communication between Danvers and the other two. The partial print pulled from Chloe's phone had come back as not belonging to either Bishop or Adams, which also gave credence to the idea that it was likely Danvers.

With his print, DNA pulled from the masks, phone records, and whatever they would find after, they were certain they would have enough direct physical evidence to convict him of his involvement in at least the captivity and rape of multiple victims.

Why? That was the big question. Over his years working for the FBI and interviewing lunatics on death row, Ben had stopped asking why they did it.

Of course he could give the psychological version. The one he taught at universities and police departments but the fact was, the mind of a predator functioned differently than that of someone with compassion for others. And so understanding them was difficult for anyone who couldn't fathom inflicting terror on another human being.

But to them, it was just another ordinary day.

It was the reason why scientists wanted to examine the

brains of murderers. It was the reason why psychologists probed them and wrote lengthy study papers about living in the mind of a monster. Everyone wanted to understand why. They want to boil it down into a palatable and acceptable conclusion if only to create a them-and-us mentality.

Why did Bundy, a seemingly charming and well-educated man, kidnap, rape, and kill his victims? Even returning to their graves to have sex with their decomposed bodies?

There was no answer — at least none that would satisfy.

People would always come to their own conclusions. Something that would help them sleep at night and allow them to place distance between themselves and those they said were insane.

For the truth was too terrifying to bear. Which was to accept that everyone had a darkness to them. It was just that serial killers explored it, got used to it, and then found gratification in it.

Ben squeezed the bridge of his nose, pushing unthinkable thoughts from his mind.

I'm coming, Chloe…. The horror of his past had come back to haunt him. Even if it wasn't Henri Bruns. At least this time he wasn't going in alone. He stared across at four strapping members of the SWAT team. Geared up in black, their trigger fingers resting alongside their weapons. Their faces a picture of concentration and focus.

The AS365 Dauphin twin-engine helicopter hovered over the middle of a highway five miles from the location. Waiting below were two cruisers blocking either side of the road. As soon as the tires kissed the road, and they felt the cushion, Ben hopped out. Wind from the blades whipped at his coat as he crouched and dashed towards a waiting cruiser. Sirens screamed, and lights flashed as they exploded out of there. Within minutes they saw the weathered sign for the turnoff down a rural road that sliced into dense woodland and wound its way around a hilly landscape. He only prayed that they would make it there before it was too late.

Chapter 50

Chief Danvers? His eyes fell on Chloe and then on the hammer in her hand.

"It's okay, sweetheart, you're safe now."

Still terrified, she took a cautionary step back.

"Where's my father?"

"He's on the way."

"Why are you alone?" she said, looking around him for any sign of another officer.

There were none.

He paused for a second as though contemplating the answer. It was enough of a hesitation to make her doubt him. Then when he didn't reply, she swallowed hard. Her mind was telling her one thing but her gut was saying something else. He was a police officer. The chief, for god's sake! But then Douglas was a ranger. How many of the other women had been taken in by trusting a badge?

He motioned with his arm. "Come on, I'll take you to

your father."

Chloe wanted to say "you are lying" but no words came out. Her mouth opened then closed. All she could muster was a head shake.

"Look, I know you've been through a lot but…"

His words faded as her mind processed not what he was saying but the way he was saying it. There was something very familiar about the tone of his voice. Then, as he gestured again with his left arm, her eyes spotted the black tattoo of the ram on his inner wrist.

It was him. He was the one in the room. The man wearing the mask. At least one of them. She wanted to turn and bolt up the stairs but he had a gun. She wouldn't have made it a few steps. No, she had to play this smart. Make him believe that she trusted him.

"Is he out there?" she muttered, hoping to convince him that her nerves were warranted. That she feared for her life. Not from him but from Douglas. Her palms were sweating, and her throat felt dry even though she had guzzled water only minutes earlier.

Fifteen feet away from her, his hand moved to his sidearm as he began closing the gap.

"No, he's not out there. Like I said, you're safe, Chloe."

"Okay," she said, her knuckles turning white as her grip tightened on the hammer's wooden handle.

"I just need to get something." She turned to head back up the stairs, trying her best to remain casual, but he wasn't buying it. He shot forward, and she stumbled trying to climb the stairs. Her shin smashed into the edge, taking her breath away. But it was too late, he had a grip on her good ankle. She tried kicking with the other foot but he blocked that fast. Her fingers raked the steps, desperately trying to pry free of his grasp, but it was useless.

One sharp twist and she drove the hammer against the side of his head. He screamed in pain and released her.

"You fucking bitch."

Chloe knew panic in its purest form in that moment. *Run!* she told herself. She would have moved past him if she thought there was a chance of not being shot in the back, instead she ran up the stairs. Blood pumping in her ears, searing pain coursing through her body. Behind her all she could hear was him cursing and saying what he was going to do.

She scrambled towards the thin strand of rope that hung loosely from the attic door. Unlike most attic stairs that folded down slowly, these stairs shot down fast, almost hitting her in the drop.

The chief's groans of agony were mixed with bursts of rage as she heard him stagger up the stairs. Capable of only limping before, she was now shifting gears with terror fueling each step. She didn't want to die, not like this. Not after all the trouble of getting out of that basement. It couldn't end like this.

The horror of not knowing if she would survive filled her with dread unlike anything she had ever experienced. He had a gun, she had a hammer.

"Chloe!" he screamed as she pulled up the stairs behind her, hoping to prevent him from following or at least slow his pursuit. Unfortunately, there was nothing to lock it with.

She now found herself enveloped in darkness. The only light came from a wooden attic eyebrow vent at the far end. *I can get out.* With adrenaline pushing her on and the sound of his voice terrifying her, she took her first step towards freedom only to lose her footing and go right through the ceiling.

Chapter 51

The weather was working against them. Storm clouds had unleashed such a downpour that the soil had shifted and become like quicksand. The cruiser engine roared as they burst over a rise and hydroplaned on the wet and slushy narrow road. Needle pine trees on either side of the road, instantly threatened to end them. It was hard to tell where the road began or ended as they snaked their way through the thick forest. All of it had become a slick death trap.

"Can't this car go any faster?" Ben shouted over the noise of the siren. It was deafening. His only hope was that Danvers would hear it and think twice. The officer driving had already been white-knuckling it, sweating and trying to see through heavy rain pounding the windshield. Ben shot a glance in the side mirror. Behind them three more cruisers and an EMS vehicle were all suffering from the same trouble as them. The waterlogged road was showing no mercy.

"If I go any faster we are going to be in a ditch or wrapped around a tree."

No sooner had he said that than he lost control of the vehicle. The ABS brakes kicked in, creating a clunking sound, but there was little that could be done to stop them from certain disaster.

Ben gripped the side of the door hard as they spun wildly out of control. Now officers were trained for this. They were meant to be prepared for the unexpected but not this time.

The collision with the tree was brutal. The driver's side was hit the hardest causing the windows to smash. As air bags inflated, a cloud of dust went everywhere. And like any good car pileup, the next two followed suit, missing them by a matter of two feet but coming to a grinding halt, caked up with dirt and stuck in the mud. The third cruiser and EMS were the fortunate ones. They had managed to slow down but they wouldn't be getting past this mess anytime soon.

The officer beside him was bleeding badly and unconscious. Ben sat there for a moment trying to get his bearings. EMS were the first to open his door. He pushed his way out his side and fell into thick slimy mud. Other officers were already rushing over to help. Ben pulled his Glock and staggered to his feet, only to buckle from pain in his side.

Only the thought of what might happen to Chloe if he didn't make it gave him strength to get back up. He told the officers who weren't involved in the crash to follow him as he broke away into the tree line. They would need to haul ass through the forest by foot.

Crushing disappointment mingled with shock and fear pushed him forward as they followed the road by cutting through the woods.

Chapter 52

Her own scream scared her more than the fall. The only reason she survived was because her arms had hooked onto a thick wooden beam. Pain coursed through her like venom. By the time she pulled herself free he was already up on the landing, and that's when it turned really bad.

At first it was two shots then three rounds that blasted through the ceiling, then he must have unloaded his entire gun because when it stopped she could hear him unloading and slamming in a second magazine.

Small shards of light lit up the roof above her. She groaned and writhed around in agonizing pain. One of the bullets had torn through her thigh.

Hot searing pain now became her world.

Still, even with her body going into shock, her will to live was stronger. She got back up again, stumbled across the beams, her mind staying focused on the attic vents.

You are going to die here, she thought.

Even if she got out, he would catch up with her and it would be over. Did anyone else know she was here? How would anyone find her?

When she reached the vents, she screamed out her frustration and anger to a deserted property. Behind her the door to the attic dropped. Light flooded the far end. She harnessed what strength was left and began kicking at the wooden vents. She wished she still had the hammer, but she'd dropped it in the fall.

Heart leaping, she knocked out two of the vents but stumbled from the pain.

"Chloe. Come on now, there's nowhere to go," his voice echoed, a reminder that if she didn't get out he was going to kill her, who knew what else he would do. She pulled herself up, gripped the edge of the structure, and continued smashing the vents with her heel as he made his way up the ladder.

Once the vents were gone, she glanced back one final time before launching herself out. She hit the roof hard and rolled, sliding down the slick surface while the sound of bullets snapped above her. Seconds of groping for anything to slow her descent and then she bounced over the edge and dropped into a large thicket of bushes. It cushioned the fall but not enough. The blow was hard and unexpected. Winded and gasping for air, she gripped her side while rain drenched through her clothes in a matter of seconds. She didn't have the luxury of catching a breath. She was up and double-timing it with a swollen, bloodied leg across the property.

If I can just get into the tree line, she told herself.

Chloe hit the ground in an awkward sprint, hobbled and pitifully limped while wincing in pain with every step. Taking in her surroundings, she was disoriented. There was no way of knowing where she was or even if there were any other homes in the area.

"Chloe!" she heard the snap of bullets before her name. By the time he burst out the rear door she already had a hundred-yard lead. She looked back and saw him begin to give chase.

Without a phone, with no idea of where a road was, all she could do was seek cover in the forest. Perhaps she could lose him. It was dense and darker than it was outside of it as heavy rain clouds had pushed out what little blue sky remained.

As she veered into the woods, the smell of pine and wet bark filled her nostrils. She forged forward into the forest, casting a glance over her shoulder one final time to see him wipe out in the mud. She wanted to gloat but there was no time. The atrocious weather gave her an additional advantage. She limped on, praying to live.

Chapter 53

Move it! One foot in front of the other, Ben ignored his thighs protesting.

His lungs were an inferno as he and four of the SWAT team emerged from the dense forest and the small log cabin came into view. By now, all five of them were flat-out sprinting. They'd heard the gunfire long before they broke out of the tree line. Alert, gun at the ready, Ben couldn't get there fast enough. The team was prepared for an all-out war. They couldn't tell where the shots originated from, inside or outside of the house. Parked nearby was Danvers's cruiser. SWAT instantly bulldozed through the front door while Ben circled around back.

He raised his gun directly in front of him. His eyes scanned the back door, windows, and roof. That's when he saw broken pieces from the attic eyebrow vent scattered on the metallic roof. Rainwater gushed over the brim of the eavestrough and a harsh wind howled.

As he approached the rear door, he heard the crack of distant gunfire coming from the forest. He glanced over his shoulder and made a mad dash for the forest line.

Don't kill her.... Don't...

Ben hurdled over a sun-bleached log and vaulted into the dark forest. He stared intensely ahead trying to make out what direction to go in. The tall pines created a canopy that strained light sporadically on the ground beneath him, making it difficult to navigate over the rough terrain.

Chapter 54

Chloe fled through the forest, stumbling over tree roots and hidden rocks.

Wheezing, she ducked behind a tree, desperate to catch her breath. Her heart was smashing against her chest as she listened to him calling out to her.

"Chloe, this could have ended differently."

He wasn't going to stop coming after her, and if he caught her she was dead. Her foot stepped on a collection of small dead tree limbs laying nearby. The snap was followed by a crack of a gun as he fired and tree bark exploded near her face.

Rising, she hit the ground running. Threading in and out of trees, stumbling forward and limping on in excruciating pain, she couldn't tell if she was going further in or looping back around. Every direction looked the same. Her injured thigh was screaming for her to stop running, but she couldn't. More difficult than moving forward was trying to control her panic.

She felt like an animal being hunted.

Another gunshot.

Her mind spun into overdrive. He was aiming at her. The thought of being shot again, or worse — being caught by him — chilled her.

So many thoughts rushed through her mind as she considered these could be her final moments alive. All the things she hadn't said to her father. The times spent with her mother and Adam. That was all that mattered to her. Not what she wanted to become. Not what she didn't have in her life; only her family.

She was so preoccupied by zipping around trees and dodging a flurry of bullets that she wasn't paying attention to what lay ahead. Acting entirely on the will to survive, she vaulted over a log while casting a glance behind her. It was a huge mistake. The ground disappeared beneath and she let out a cry. Landing, she slipped down a steep, mossy incline, grasping for anything to slow her descent. Head over heels she twisted and turned, flattening thin upright plants, saplings, and brambles until she crashed into a tree trunk. Her face bruised and cut, she gripped her side certain that a rib had broken. Each inhale was as painful as the next.

I have to hide... I need to catch my breath... just a few seconds... Dazed, she crawled on her belly, clawing at the wet soil until she made it behind a large boulder. Above, further up the slope, she heard him getting closer. The sound of undergrowth rustling, and rage could be heard.

"There's nowhere to hide, Chloe. I will find you."

In the silence of the forest his voice seemed louder than it should. Wherever she was, there couldn't have been other homes nearby. It would've been a huge risk chasing a woman and yelling. She squeezed her mouth closed trying to stop her hot breath from giving away her location. The heavy rain turned the ground into mush. She waited until his footsteps moved on before she ventured out. Even then she was hesitant to move.

Frozen, exhausted, and applying pressure to her wound, she knew if she didn't get out of this forest she would likely bleed to death. Planting her good leg, she pushed on and scrambled up the embankment, crunching underbrush and pulling on tree roots to get her to the top.

She had only got maybe twenty feet before a hand grabbed her. Her muffled cry was silenced instantly. Her eyes bulged for a few seconds with a sense of dread that he had her.

"Quiet, Chloe."

"Dad?"

Chapter 55

For Ben and Chloe, the reunion was short-lived. There was so much that he wanted to say but there was no time. With his back pressed against a trunk he kept a firm grip on her as he risked a glance around the tree.

"Now listen to me carefully. There is a SWAT team back at the house. In a minute I want you to run."

She nodded, understanding the gravity of the situation. Ben could see Danvers in the distance, searching the forest. Once he saw him disappear down an incline he released his grip.

"Don't stop. Don't look back. No matter what, you get to them. Now go. Run!"

Chloe bolted, partially limping. He saw the wound and felt an uncontrollable anger. He kept his eyes on Danvers, only glancing a couple of times to make sure Chloe was still moving. Satisfied, he stepped out from behind the tree and approached Danvers. When he got within twenty yards and had him fixed within his sights, Danvers wheeled around.

"Put it down," Ben said. "It's over."

He chuckled a little, glancing around the forest as though he was checking to see if there were any others. "That kid of yours is strong, Ben. She'd make a good cop."

Ben didn't reply. All he focused on was the gun in his hand.

"Tell me, how did you find out?"

"You, Douglas, and Ted were at every crime scene. You were the only ones who could get close to them without campers batting an eye. You abused your position of authority. Covered up, pushed the investigation in the direction you wanted it go. You had Douglas come in. You called in that abduction after you told Ted to grab another. You shot Ted and placed Douglas in that cell knowing full well he would kill himself. Or perhaps you did it?"

"You are reaching. All circumstantial."

"Is it? We'll let the court decide. I'm certain the partial

print from the cell phone will show up as yours. The Hayes girl and my own daughter I'm sure will give them more than enough details to prove beyond a reasonable doubt that you were involved. There's DNA, testimonies, and a hunting photo showing your connection with them. No matter how you look at this, you are going away for a long time, you sick bastard."

Danvers snorted before lowering his sidearm. He nodded slowly and got this faraway look in his eyes as if he was taking one final look at freedom.

"You sanctimonious prick. Don't tell me that you wouldn't have done the same in my position," Danvers said.

Shifting blame. It was always the same.

"You want to know why?"

"No. No, I stopped needing to know a long time ago. You're all the same. Monsters."

Flanking him, several of the SWAT team arrived.

He smirked and gave a curt bow upon seeing them. He looked up and inhaled deeply. "Back at the station, you said I wasn't prepared to do what was necessary."

"Put the gun down, Danvers," Ben repeated.

Brandishing his weapon, he jabbed it at the ground to drive home his point.

"I'm the only one who is prepared to do what is necessary."

Suddenly, in that instant Ben saw his hand wheeling up. Before Danvers could pull the trigger, Ben unloaded three rounds in his chest and one in the head.

He flew backwards, landing hard. Then there was silence. It was finally over.

The decision to go out shooting instead of handing himself in might not have been smart, but his life was over. Danvers knew he wouldn't have survived inside a lockup. Two SWAT guys moved in on him while Ben turned to see Chloe standing nearby with the others. Tears streaked as he rushed over and gripped her tightly. She held onto him for dear life, sobbing into his neck. She might have been seventeen, but she was still his little girl. That would never change.

Epilogue

Ben sat down on his private dock, sunglasses pushed back and his feet dangling in the cool bay water. He was enjoying the last few days of summer. A warm band of sunshine bathed his face as he breathed in the salty air. The leaves had already begun to change into golden colors. Lobster boats bobbed up and down in the harbor, fishermen occasionally waved to one another.

He'd grown fond of Eden Falls. The quiet, laid-back community had welcomed him. Though it had been tainted by murder and the shock of a police chief's involvement, things were starting to return to normal. The media had finally moved on to a new story. Phone calls for interviews had become less frequent and Chloe was beginning to smile again.

He settled back on the palms of his hands, basking in the beauty of Maine's coast — its rugged shoreline, and the orange sun dipping beyond the horizon.

He could get used to this if it stayed this way but it wouldn't.

It would soon turn cold. A thick blanket of snow and ice would arrive, and with that would come the need to shovel driveways, put on winter tires, and deal with below-zero temperatures. That was something he wasn't used to, coming from Florida. The very thought gave him a chill.

Perhaps he would spend his winters in Florida. He still had a place to stay. Instead of selling the small property in the Keys, he'd used it as a timeshare. It was another source of income and it gave them a reason to go back. Something they hadn't done since the death of his wife and son. Besides, Nate was still hounding him to return to the bureau.

But for Ben that was behind him. He wanted a slower pace of life and this gave him that.

Behind him he heard footsteps approaching. He twisted around to see Dakota Woods holding two bottles of beer. He'd invited her over for a BBQ. Janice and a few of Chloe's friends had shown up. She was dressed in shorts, T-shirt, and flip-flops.

"That beer I owe you."

He removed his shades, giving a small boyish grin.

"Isn't that from my fridge?"

"Yeah. Don't ever say I'm not resourceful." She smirked and took a seat beside him. He placed his beer down. Beads of condensation formed a ring on the wooden dock.

"So you didn't take Nate up on his offer, I see."

"No, I thought I would stick around a while."

"And step on the next chief's toes?"

"Someone's got to do it. By the way, has the town manager made a decision yet?"

"Not so far. I don't think they are in a rush this time." She paused to sip from her bottle. "Maybe you should apply."

He chuckled. "Me?"

"Why not? You've got experience."

"You got to be joking. I'm no one's whipping boy.

Especially a bunch of uptight council members."

"Oh, there's good benefits."

He laughed. "I think I'll stick to teaching."

"How's Chloe?" she asked.

Ben watched a group of seagulls break from the water. "She's getting better. Her leg is healing up nicely."

"Therapy?" Dakota asked.

"Yeah, still once a week with Dr. Rose."

"You like Emily?"

He shot her a sideways glance. "Who's asking?"

"Oh, enquiring minds. You know how this town is, everyone loves to gossip."

He hesitated before replying. "Maybe I'm interested in someone else."

"Really? Do tell."

"No, a man has to have some secrets. By the way, how's your shoulder?"

She sipped her beer. "Oh it's still giving me a few aches. Next time, you can take the bullet."

"There won't be a next time."

She laughed. “Forrester, of course there will. It’s in your blood.”

“Ben.”

“I’ll call you that when you stop calling me Woods.”

“Kind of goes well, don’t you think?” he asked.

“What?”

“The whole Woods and Forrester. Has a ring to it.”

“Yeah, maybe we should start a traveling circus.”

They both laughed.

* * *

A week later, Ben was reading out in the sunroom when Chloe came in.

“You’re back early?”

“Decided I would stay in for the night,” she replied.

“Yeah? And do what?”

“Watch a movie with you. Maybe we can pick out an old ’80s flick.”

She had always loved them. Something about that era suited her. Ben told her she should have grown up in the ’80s.

"Sounds like a plan. I'll wrestle us up some popcorn, you find the movie."

Ben went out to the kitchen and rooted through the cupboard for the box of popcorn. His eyes fell on a bottle of scotch on the counter. His mouth watered and for a few seconds he considered having a glass. He gave it a rain check. He hadn't given it up, but he was trying to wean himself off it. At least, to the point of where he wasn't relying on it to cope.

He hadn't heard from Henri Bruns since the calls he'd received while investigating.

Occasionally the phone would ring in the night but it was usually a telemarketer. It still bothered him to know that he was out there. But some part of him got a feeling that Bruns wouldn't show his face or come after him or his daughter. Not because he respected Ben or even admired him, but he wouldn't risk getting caught. That's what made him different to others. He wasn't in it for the fame. He wasn't trying to rack up a body count so he could boast in prison. Had Ben not stumbled across his heinous acts, he would have still been taking women in the Everglades.

Was it over between them? Only time would tell. Nate had suggested moving again but where would that get him? If Bruns wanted to kill him, he would have done it by now. As it stood, Ben wasn't going to let him or anyone rob him of enjoying life.

He poured some ice tea and listened to the popcorn explode inside the microwave like firecrackers. The aroma of butter reaching his nostrils made his stomach grumble. He glanced at the photo of Elizabeth and Adam. He missed them. Both of them did.

Carrying out the popcorn in a large bowl and juggling two glasses, he heard a knock at the door. Chloe bolted up and answered it.

"Dad, it's for you."

Ben shuffled out to find Dakota standing in the doorway with a police file in her hand.

"There's been a murder, you think you can look this over?"

"Please tell me it's not related to the last case?"

"No, this is something entirely different."

He squeezed the bridge of his nose, feeling a headache coming on. "Come on in, Woods."

* * *

THANK YOU FOR READING

The Second book in the 50 States of Murder will be available in June 2020.

Please take a second to leave a review, it's really appreciated. Thanks kindly, Jon.

NEWSLETTER

Thank you for buying Lost Girls: The Maine Murders

Building a relationship with readers is one of the best things about writing. I occasionally send out a newsletter with details on new releases and subscriber only special offers. For instance, with each new release of a book, you will be alerted to it at a subscriber only discounted rate.

Go here to receive special offers, bonus content, and news about Jon's new books, sign up for the newsletter. http://www.jonmills.com/

A PLEA...

If you enjoyed the book, I would really appreciate it if you would consider leaving a review. I can't stress how helpful this is in helping other readers decide if they should give it a shot. Reviews from readers like you are the best recommendation a book can have. Without reviews, an author's books are virtually invisible on the retail sites. It also lets me know what you liked. You can leave a review by visiting the book's page. I would greatly appreciate it. It only takes a couple of seconds.

Thank you — **Jon Mills**

JON MILLS

Jon Mills is originally from England. He currently lives in Ontario, Canada with his family. He is the author of The Debt Collector series, 50 States of Murder Thrillers, The Promise, True Connection, I'm Still Here, and the Undisclosed Trilogy. To get more information about upcoming books or if you wish to get in touch with Jon, you can do so using the following contact information:

Twitter: Jon_Mills

Facebook: authorjonmills

Website: www.jonmills.com

Email: contact@jonmills.com

Made in the USA
San Bernardino, CA
08 April 2020

67471744R00239